IN THE GRIP OF DEATH!

Sheer panic flooded through the Gunsmith as he felt Elwin's arm clamp around his ribs and start to crush them. Clint knew there was no hope for escape. Clint's fingers clawed for Elwin's knife sheathed at his belt. He found the handle, and somehow, he managed to tear it free. With the bones in his ribs and his neck practically popping like corks, Clint stabbed Elwin with the bowie knife. Stabbed him again and again as the man bellowed and tried to break his neck. . . .

DON'T MISS THESE
ALL-ACTION WESTERN SERIES
FROM THE BERKLEY PUBLISHING GROUP

THE GUNSMITH by J. R. Roberts
> Clint Adams was a legend among lawmen, outlaws, and ladies. They called him . . . the Gunsmith.

LONGARM by Tabor Evans
> The popular long-running series about U.S. Deputy Marshal Long—his life, his loves, his fight for justice.

LONE STAR by Wesley Ellis
> The blazing adventures of Jessica Starbuck and the martial arts master, Ki. Over eight million copies in print.

SLOCUM by Jake Logan
> Today's longest-running action Western. John Slocum rides a deadly trail of hot blood and cold steel.

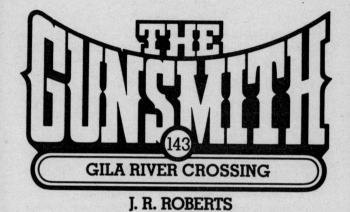

THE GUNSMITH

143

GILA RIVER CROSSING

J. R. ROBERTS

JOVE BOOKS, NEW YORK

GILA RIVER CROSSING

A Jove Book / published by arrangement with
the author

PRINTING HISTORY
Jove edition / November 1993

ISBN: 0-515-11240-2

A JOVE BOOK®
Jove Books are published by The Berkley Publishing Group,
200 Madison Avenue, New York, New York 10016.
JOVE and the "J" design are trademarks
belonging to Jove Publications, Inc.

PRINTED IN THE UNITED STATES OF AMERICA

10 9 8 7 6 5 4 3 2 1

ONE

It was hotter than blazes when Clint Adams followed the Gila River up into the mountains of western New Mexico with one eye out for raiding Apache and the other for a town where he could earn some honest wages. Duke, his big, black gelding, was dragging his head low and was as gaunt as a desert coyote from all the hard riding they'd done across the Sonoran Desert. And between the Apache and the terrible Arizona heat, both man and horse were played out and worn down to a nubbin.

The hard climb off the desert floor wasn't easy, but at least the air was cooling with the higher altitude and the Gila River ran swift and clear. Three days of climbing brought them to the crest of a mountain ridge where Clint had a commanding vista of a great mountain valley below. At the north edge of the huge valley was the prettiest ranching and mining town he'd seen in a long, long time.

"That must be Big Pine," he told the gelding as he scratched its ears. "And I'll just bet they need a gunsmith with my talents and that they have a good stall with plenty of green grass for a tired horse like you, Duke."

The gelding flicked its ears and nickered.

Clint was coated with dust and dried sweat and knew he smelled worse than a rutting boar hog. As he reined his gelding down the trail toward Big Pine, the Gunsmith dug his hands into his pockets and drew out the last of his cash.

He counted the money and muttered, "Four dollars and change, Duke. That's a pretty sorry accounting for all the scrapes and fixes we've fought through over the last several years. About enough for couple nights room and board. I'm either going to have to find a poker game and some luck, or else set up shop right away and take in some honest cash. Which do you think?"

The horse just kept plodding down the mountainside. It was as if Duke understood that it did not matter what he thought because the Gunsmith was going to do whatever he wanted to do anyway.

"Well," Clint said, cramming the wadded bills back into his jeans, "I guess we'll just have to see what kind of a reception we get in Big Pine before I decide how to proceed. One thing for sure—I can't afford to lose even a damn dollar at cards. Let's just hope that Big Pine don't already have a couple of first-rate gunsmiths scratchin' for a living."

Halfway down the mountain, Clint cut across a wagon track and rode about a mile until he came across a couple of miners. They were about a hundred yards above the road and hauling rock out of a mine tunnel.

"Howdy!" Clint called in greeting.

The miners stopped their work. One of them patted the six-gun at his side, and it said more than words that they weren't interested in idle conversation. Clint understood that, but some inner perversity made him ignore the obvious message.

"Now how'd you know that I was the best damn gun-smith in the country?" he called, reining Duke to a stand-still and grinning broadly.

"Git on outta here!" the larger of the two bellowed. "This here is our mining claim."

"How about that?" Clint said, thumbing his hat back. "Is it rich?"

"That'd be none of your business!"

"Well, maybe not," Clint answered, "but if you're makin' money you better have a good side arm to protect your claim. And that *is* my business. I'll be setting up a shop in that little town yonder. Stop on by, and I'll clean and oil that hog leg you're wearing. Probably don't shoot straight unless it's been worked on lately."

The big man snarled and drew his six-gun. He aimed at Clint and shouted, "You're a damn smart aleck! I got no use for—"

Clint's hand streaked to the well-oiled Colt at his side. It came up faster than the strike of a snake and belched fire and smoke. The big miner bellowed in pain and his gun went flying off into the mine tailings he'd just dumped.

"Well, now," Clint said with a grin, "I guess you *do* need a good gunsmith after all. Look me up in Big Pine, gents!"

The two miners gaped until Clint holstered his gun and rode slowly on down the mountainside, a happy whistle on his lips.

"Nothing wrong with being friendly and creating a little business for yourself at the same time," he told his weary gelding.

Big Pine was bustling and looked prosperous. It was located right on the banks of the Gila, and the town's main street had an air of confidence and permanence. Clint couldn't imagine why, seeing as how the Apache still ruled these mountains and it was common knowledge that their raids were frequent and bloody. But in the town itself, people seemed unaware of the Apache presence. Clint saw a sheriff's office, a stone bank, and even a small newspaper office, a sure sign that the town took itself seriously.

There were four saloons, all of them wooden instead of just tent canvas. There was a saddle shop, a blacksmith shop, and two big liveries. Clint rode Duke right up to the one at the south end of Big Pine and dismounted. An old man and a barefoot boy came out to greet him. The old man might have been in his eighties. He had a tobacco-stained beard and hands like hams. Once, he'd been a big man, but now he was frail and bent, yet his eyes were clear and penetrating. The boy was cut of the same cloth, and there was such a strong resemblance between them that Clint was sure that they were grandpa and grandson.

"Howdy, mister!" the boy called, his blue eyes crinkled over freckled cheeks. "You come a long, hard way."

"That's right," Clint said, "we have. All the way from over by the Colorado River and a place called Yuma. Followed the Gila River to these high mountains."

"What fer?" the old man asked.

"Just seemed like the natural thing to do," Clint answered. "I like to travel and so does my horse."

"He looks plumb traveled into the ground."

"You don't look so perky yourself, old-timer," Clint said with an easy smile which brought the old man up short and caused the kid to grin.

"Your horse needs heavy graining," the kid said. "Cost you a little extra, but this horse looks to be a good one. I'd buy the grain, mister."

"Well," Clint said, "how *much* extra?"

"Dime a day."

"What's your name?"

The boy, who looked to be about twelve, hitched up his britches and said, "Dan Hurley. This here is my grandpa, Dud Hurley."

"Dan and Dud," Clint said. "Sounds like a good team to me."

"My pa was named Don Hurley," the boy announced proudly. "Everyone in Big Pine knows we're scrappy but damned good workers. Honest, too. You'll get more than a dime's worth of grain a day here, mister."

Clint liked the way this boy stated things straight-out, and he believed what he said about the Hurley family. "Well, here's two dollars. Feed 'im and grain 'im as long as the money lasts. By then, maybe I'll have earned or won some more cash and we'll see about things."

"You lookin' for livery work, we ain't got none," Dud Hurley said. "Boy and me handles all of it."

"Actually," Clint said, "I'm a gunsmith. You got one working in Big Pine?"

"Big Al Mintner is the sheriff, and he does some gunsmithin' on the side to keep himself in beer. He ain't worth much either sheriffin' or gunsmithin', but I'd not want to be the man who tries to take away his business."

"I see," Clint mused. "Well, this here is a free country, and a man with an honest trade ought to feel he can open up a shop wherever he pleases. If he's better than the competition, the word will get around and he'll prosper. I have always prospered at gunsmithing and beat out the competition. Big Al is just going to have to step aside."

"The sheriff don't step aside for anybody, mister," the boy said. "Might be healthier to keep that two dollars and move onto another town if you're going to be stubborn about gunsmithing."

Clint frowned and handed his reins to the boy but looked at the old man. "Dud, I've sheriffed some myself. It was always my understanding that a lawman was supposed to serve and protect the honest citizens of his town. Sounds to me like this Sheriff Mintner has sort of got things backward."

"You see which way the smoke drifts real quick, don't you?" the old man said. "That being the case, maybe you'll understand real quick that it ain't healthy to buck the sheriff. The nearest town is about seventy miles northeast. It's called Socorro. Far as I know, their sheriff just sheriffs."

Clint shook his head with a tired grin. "I like Big Pine just fine, Mr. Hurley. And I expect you'd like to keep my two dollars and put some weight back on my worn-out gelding. So where I can get a room?"

"Fancy or plain?"

"Plain. Real plain and cheap."

"Helldorado Hotel is two bits a night," the old man said, pointing to a two-story hotel down the street. "Comes with cockroaches, though."

"Room and board, huh?" Clint asked with a smile. "It'll do."

Despite what seemed like his best effort, the old man chuckled. "You don't spook too easy, do you? What's your name?"

"Clint Adams."

"Holy hog fat!" Dan cried. "You're the Gunsmith!"

"I told you I was a gunsmith."

"No, *the* Gunsmith!"

Clint sighed. "I prefer to just go by my given name, son. I'm not a lawman, a bounty hunter, or a fast gun. I'm just a man a little down on his luck lookin' for a place to rest up and earn an honest dollar."

"You could sleep in our barn," Dan said, looking to his grandfather. "Couldn't he?"

When the old man hesitated, the boy cried, "Grandpa, he's famous!"

"He's damn near broke," the man said. "But if you want, Clint, you can sleep in a stall. Be fine with us."

"Much obliged," Clint said. "If I don't do some gunsmithing business or find myself a lucky card game, I may want to do that tomorrow night. But tonight, I've got my heart set on a regular bed, a shave, and a bath. I'll be back in tomorrow morning to let you know how my plans are progressing."

Clint grabbed up his saddlebags and started off down the street. But the boy rushed up and said, "You really want us to keep your real name a secret?"

"I just want to be left alone and treated like everyone else," Clint said.

"If you cross Sheriff Mintner, the sparks will fly. He's real quick with a shooter, Mr. Adams. Probably not as quick as you, but he's sneaky as a fox. He gets to be your enemy, you'd best watch your back."

"I always do," Clint said. "But I've no quarrel with any sheriff. They're always underpaid and expected to do too damn much. I'm sure that your sheriff and I will get along just fine."

"You will as long as he don't find you gunsmithing in Big Pine," the boy warned before he turned and shuffled back to the livery.

Clint stopped in his tracks and turned to look at the boy as he walked away. Dan Hurley's words troubled him; he wondered just what kind of sheriff ran this town. Apparently, one that made his own set of rules and made sure

that they filled his own pockets. That was sad. Clint had
enjoyed a long and distinguished career as a lawman, and
he still carried his old badge with pride. Therefore, when
he ran across an officer whose primary reason for being
in office was profit, it was damned upsetting.

Clint turned and continued on toward the Helldorado
Hotel. He was nearing it when he saw a big man wearing
a tin sheriff's badge emerge from a café with the prettiest
little gal that Clint had seen in a long time. As the big sheriff escorted the woman down the street, citizens cleared
the boardwalk with a smile because the blonde was so
pretty.

Clint stepped up into their path and tipped his hat to the
woman. Their eyes met and locked. The blonde smiled at
him, and when Clint smiled back, he thought he saw a
little blush color her cheeks.

"Step aside, saddle tramp," the sheriff growled, not
liking anyone to catch his girl's eye.

Clint had no intention of stepping aside, and maybe the
pretty blonde saw that because she pulled the sheriff into
a millinery shop before there was a confrontation. But not
before the sheriff gave Clint a hard look of warning. Clint
just deflected that warning right back.

No question about it, the Gunsmith thought as he continued on toward the hotel, Big Pine was a nice town
with a bad sheriff. Maybe Al Mintner just needed a lesson in humility. And maybe that buxom little blonde
with the pretty smile and hourglass figure needed a new
boyfriend.

Clint decided it was definitely worth staying around to
find out.

TWO

The lobby of the Helldorado Hotel was littered with ciga-
rette butts and soaked with tobacco juice. There wasn't a
cuspidor in sight, only plenty of rough-looking men who
eyed Clint suspiciously when he stepped inside carrying
his saddlebags, Winchester rifle, and gunsmithing tools.
The hotel lobby reeked of vomit and unwashed bodies.
Flies swarmed, and a drunk was lying facedown on the
floor, snoring.

Jesus, Clint thought, stepping over the drunk and ignoring the hard looks cast in his direction by the motley
crowd, what a pigsty!

The hotel desk clerk didn't even bother to look up from
his newspaper when Clint dropped his bags on the floor
and leaned on the registration desk. Instead, the man said,
"Two bits a night, in advance."

Clint reached into his jeans and laid the money on the
desk. "Which room?"

"Just a minute while I finish this article," the man
drawled, still not looking up from behind his newspaper.

Clint's hand snapped out and seized the paper. He tore
it from the clerk's grasp and then grabbed the surprised
man by the shirtfront and dragged him right up onto the

9

desk. The clerk was in his mid-forties, thin and dirty. He looked like a cornered ferret as the Gunsmith cocked back his fist.

"When I talk to a man, I expect him to talk back to me, eyeball to damned eyeball!"

"Yes, sir!" the desk clerk screeched. "Room twenty-two is available."

"Is it clean? With fresh sheets and a pitcher of water?"

One look into the desk clerk's frightened face told the Gunsmith that Room 22 was neither clean nor ready for his occupancy. "Git up there and clean it up for me," he snarled as he threw the man back against the wall. "Now!"

The clerk grabbed a broom, two laundered sheets from under the desk, and a water pitcher. He jumped past Clint and bounded up the stairs as laughter erupted in the lobby.

Clint turned to regard the other patrons, and he wasn't smiling. "You people are a bunch of pigs! Find brooms, mops, and buckets and clean this barnyard up right now!"

The laughter died. Two of the largest men looked around, found support, and stepped forward to confront the Gunsmith. One, a heavyset man with bad teeth and a scraggly black beard said, "Mister, you already had your fun with Ernie. He's a prideful little bastard and deserved what you gave him. But this is different. We don't take orders from no man."

Clint was tired and irritable. If he could have, he'd have just said to hell with it and picked up his bags and found a clean hotel. But this was all he could afford tonight, and he'd be damned if he'd walk over drunks and be a part of such trashiness.

"What're your names?" Clint asked.

"Huh?"

Clint forced a hard smile. "You and your skinny, lice-ridden friend. What are your names?"

The big man glanced sideways at his partner, a tall, ugly man with a bad knife scar across his right cheek. The man growled, "My name is Horse Davis. This here is Hank. And if you don't grab up your gear and get your ass outta this hotel, we're going to kick it and you all the way down the street."

"Well, Horse, let's just see how you're going to do that."

Horse glanced sideways at Hank and an unspoken agreement passed between them a moment before they charged the Gunsmith. Clint hadn't been a lawman for half his lifetime without learning a few things. Number one was that you did not brawl with brawlers. Do that and you'd take a pounding and, even if you won, you'd probably bust up your hands so that they were useless for shuckin' a gun.

Clint drew his Colt, and its heavy barrel cracked across the forehead of Horse, dropping him like a stone. Hank was quicker and managed to land a solid punch that rocked Clint backward on his heels. Clint ducked a second punch and stabbed the barrel of his Colt into Hank's throat. The tall, angular man's eyes bulged. His mouth began to open and close like that of a fish pulled out of water. After a moment he turned blue, and his eyes reflected his terror.

"Jesus Christ!" a man shouted. "He's gonna strangle to death before our eyes!"

"No, he won't," Clint said, holstering his gun. "He's going to *look* like he's strangling, but he'll manage a whisper of breath."

The other patrons gaped in morbid fascination as Hank sank to his knees, both hands clutching his throat as he made little squeaks, sucking for air. Clint stepped around the desk to open a small broom closet where he found brooms, mops, and buckets. They were draped in cobwebs.

"Here!" he shouted, tossing the cleaning gear over the desk to the other patrons. "Get to work, unless someone else has contrary ideas."

"What about Horse?" one of the men asked, catching a broom. "He's out cold, and he's gonna get sick when he wakes."

"Then toss him out into the alley. If I were the sheriff of this town, I'd throw him in jail, and when he sobered up, I'd give him the choice of acting like a man or getting out of Big Pine."

"Who the hell *are* you?" another man asked, still watching Hank clutching his throat with bulging, terrified eyes.

"I'm Clint Adams, and the reason I'm here is that I'm down on my luck, same as the rest of you. But just because things are a little rough at the moment is no reason why we can't live like men instead of barnyard animals. Right?."

The roomful of saddle tramps and drunks nodded.

"All right then," Clint said, "Let's get busy cleaning up this pigsty."

A few hours later when Clint descended the stairs, he was freshly shaved and bathed and was wearing the clean shirt he'd brought up to his room in his saddle-bags. He paused on the stairway and looked down at the lobby. It was still swarming with flies and reeked, but at least it was clean and there were two cuspidors on the floor beside the dilapidated sofas and overstuffed chairs. Furthermore, the other boarders appeared sober and alert.

"Everything all right now, Mr. Adams?" the desk clerk asked nervously.

"Just fine," Clint said, nodding to the other men in the lobby before he continued on down the stairs and out into the evening for a meal, a beer, and a look at downtown Big Pine.

The meal was good. For fifty cents he had a fine steak dinner, apple pie for dessert, and plenty of coffee. He would have liked a good cigar, but it was too much of an extravagance. That being the case, Clint beckoned the waitress over to his table.

"More coffee?"

"No, ma'am," he said to the woman, who looked used up and appeared to be in her late thirties. "I was just wondering which of the saloons has the best reputation."

"For what?"

"An honest card game."

She smiled and shook her head. Her hair was damp with perspiration. "Odds are always with the house, mister. Don't matter if it's here or in any other town, the house always has the edge. You're a big boy and look like you've done some livin'. You ought to know that as well as me."

Clint sighed. "Yeah, you're right. You see, I'm a little down on my luck right now."

"Aren't we all?" the woman said, taking a seat across from Clint without waiting for an invitation. There were only two other customers left in the café, and she seemed to feel they were getting along fine without her intervention. "So what are you thinking about doing to make a dollar?"

Clint told her about his gunsmithing, and she said, "That's a damn pity. Sheriff Mintner won't let you make a dime at that trade, mister. My suggestion is that you ride on out of Big Pine and try to make an honest living up in Socorro."

"I've already heard that advice from little Dan Hurley," Clint said. "Frankly, that kind of advice bothers me. I'm a man that likes to decide for myself where I'm going to do business."

The waitress studied him closely. "Mister, you've got a kind and intelligent face. I suggest you move on to Socorro and keep that face from getting bashed in by the sheriff's fist or boot. The simple fact is, no one would ever use you because they'd be afraid of angering Sheriff Mintner."

"Say now," Clint said, "that *is* troubling. Who is that pretty blond woman I saw on his arm this afternoon?"

"That's Miss Angie Buttering," the waitress replied, frowning with disapproval. "I guess she's already caught your eye."

"She'd catch any man's eye."

"Yeah," the waitress said with a trace of bitterness. "She's a tart and a flirt, but she's got the equipment to take her pick of men. She's no good, though. 'Cept for one thing."

Clint caught the waitress's meaning. "Is she a prostitute?"

"Not the kind that you'd find in a crib or working in a saloon. And I expect that she don't actually take money for her favors, but she knows how to get what she wants."

"Then why is she wasting her time with a two-bit sheriff?"

"He's not so two-bit," the waitress said. "Mintner has run off a few merchants, and he seems to find a way to buy up their shops and rent them out at a profit. I heard him brag one time that he was fixing to quit being a lawman in a couple more years and then he'd run for mayor of Big Pine and maybe take up cattle ranching."

"Cattle ranching?"

"Sure. He'll find a way to get ahold of some poor rancher's spread. Men like that take what they want and they get rich. I suspect that Miss Buttering can see the writing on the wall."

Clint frowned and finished his coffee. He stood up and dipped a hand into his pocket. He laid a dime on the table as a tip, and the waitress took it without enthusiasm or thanks.

"What's your name?" Clint asked.

She brushed back the damp tendrils of hair on her face and pushed her chest out a little. Taking a deep breath, she looked him in the eye and said, "Sarah. Miss Sarah Taylor."

"Well, Miss Sarah Taylor, thanks for your well-meaning advice."

"Where you staying?" she asked, trying to sound casual.

"At the Helldorado Hotel."

"That's a shithouse. I get off work at ten o'clock. Maybe I could help you find something . . . nicer."

Clint knew exactly what Sarah meant. And he was tempted, he had not had a woman in weeks. But the truth of the matter was that he felt the need to try his hand at cards and then to get some sleep.

"Maybe tomorrow night, if the offer is still good."

"I might have other plans."

"Then I'd be real disappointed, Miss Taylor, but I'd find some other way to amuse myself."

She chuckled. "Yeah, I expect you're the kind of man who can find lots to do, even if you are broke. I expect you've got a line for the women longer than my arm."

"Longer than your shapely leg, Miss Taylor."

Sarah pulled up her dress and placed her foot on a chair. "What do you think about that? I used to have prettier legs than Angie Buttering. And where they meet is still better."

Clint blushed, and the other two patrons gaped. Then Clint tipped his hat and strolled out the door, thinking that he would be a fool not to find out just how nice Sarah Taylor was tomorrow night.

The Boneyard Bar and Gambling Parlor had a poker game going, but the stakes were far too high for Clint so he wandered down the street until he came to the Cowboy Saloon. It was half-filled, and a banjo player was picking an unfamiliar tune while a girl in a black dress and stockings swayed on the bar top. Boisterous drinkers shamelessly rubbernecked while trying to look up her dress.

Clint moseyed through the crowd and stopped at a poker table. He watched the game for a few minutes and saw that the ante was only a dime. Clint reckoned that he had about enough money to play two hands, maybe three, and then, if he didn't win, he'd be tapped out.

"Take a seat, mister," the house gambler said with a cold smile. "Five-card draw, nothing wild."

Clint pulled up a chair. Besides himself, there were three other players in addition to the gambler. They were all cowboys, most of them barely out of their teens. Two appeared to be drunk and just about busted.

"Ante up," the gambler said, cutting the cards and then handing the deck to Clint so that he could cut them again before the deal.

The Gunsmith obliged, and when the cards were dealt, he saw that the gambler was dealing from the bottom of the deck. The cardsharp was good but not of the quality that one would find in San Francisco's better gambling establishments or on a Mississippi River paddle wheeler.

After two losing hands, Clint drew three aces and was ready to make a winning hand. "Two more cards," he intoned, drawing two cards of no value.

The bet was raised to three dollars, high stakes among working cowboys.

"I'll take two myself," the house gambler said, calling out to the bartender for beer in order to distract everyone's attention while he dealt from the bottom of the deck.

But Clint's hand clamped on his wrist, and he slammed the gambler's forearm down on the edge of the round gambling table so hard that it broke.

The gambler screamed and fumbled for a derringer in his silk vest pocket. Clint's left fist caught the gambler on the side of the jaw and sent him and his chair crashing over backward. The gambler quivered and passed out.

Clint collected the pot and then calmly regarded the other cowboys. "On a deal like this," he explained, ignoring the commotion behind the bar, "what is generally considered fair is to divide the cheater's pile of chips."

"We could do that?" one young, peach-faced cowboy asked with amazement.

"Why not?" Clint responded. "He was cheating. Those chips were won from you boys by underhanded dealing."

"Well, hot damn!" the kid said, his eyes a little glassy from all the beer he'd consumed.

But another cowboy shoved his chair back and stood up. "I'm not takin' a one of 'em! Sheriff Mintner hears we did that, we'll be in the doghouse for certain, and you know what a son of a bitch that will be."

"Yeah," the other cowboy sadly agreed.

Clint was appalled. "But it's *your* money!"

"I'm gettin' out of here. I want no trouble with the sheriff next time I ride into town."

"Me neither!"

Clint could not hide his disgust. "What about you?" he asked the glassy-eyed cowboy. "Are you also afraid to take what is yours?"

The cowboy reached out and took a couple of chips but then dropped them, whirled, and staggered away after his friends.

Clint shook his head and threw up his hands in dismay and amazement. "Well," he said to no one in particular, "I guess all these chips are mine. Lucky me!"

The Gunsmith scooped up the chips, stepped over the unconscious gambler, and sauntered over to the bar. "Cash 'em in," he ordered.

"If I do that," the bartender replied, "you'd better be on a fast horse heading out of Big Pine before Sheriff Mintner catches wind of this."

"Why? The gambler was dealing from the bottom of the deck. There are witnesses."

"None that would swear to that," the bartender said, glancing toward the swinging batwing doors where the cowboys had passed. Clint heard the pounding of hooves and knew the cowboys were beating it out of town.

Clint turned and surveyed the room. He felt anger filling his gut, and he was in a reckless mood. "We are all working men. I caught that gambler cheating your friends, and I'm taking the pot. That's only fair. But before I go, I'm buying drinks on the house. Anyone too afraid to drink free whiskey?"

The cowboys hesitated only a moment, and then one said, "We'll be drinking to your funeral, stranger."

"Drink to whatever you want," Clint said. "But I'll be drinking to my health and new prosperity."

He turned. "Bartender, cash in these chips and then set up drinks on me for everyone! My name is Clint, and I'm opening a gunsmithing business first thing tomorrow morning. I hope you all will come by and pay me a visit."

"Your funeral," the bartender said as reached under the bar for the house money and half a dozen bottles of cheap whiskey.

THREE

When Clint walked out of the Cowboy Saloon, he had more than thirty dollars in his pockets. It wasn't a fortune, but it sure was a lot more than he'd had when he'd started out looking for a card game.

"Hello."

Clint turned to see the waitress, Sarah Taylor, standing in front of the millinery shop.

"Well, hello!"

She perked up at the warmth of his greeting. "I saw three cowboys come busting out of the saloon, and before one of them could leave, I asked him what the trouble was. He said that you knocked out a gambler and claimed a big pile of poker chips."

"That's about the size of it," Clint admitted. "When I left your café, I left a dime for a tip. Now, I'm upping that to a dollar."

Clint gave her the dollar bill, knowing that it would probably be more than Sarah had earned the entire evening in tips.

Sarah beamed. "When you turn a little lucky you sure are extravagant."

"Easy come and easy go," he said, taking her arm. "Where are we going?"

"I've got a little shack at the end of town," Sarah said. "Got a bottle of whiskey and a soft pillow."

"Well," the Gunsmith said, "that sounds pretty inviting. But Sarah, you know I'm not a settling kind of man."

She paused on the shadowy boardwalk. "If you're trying to tell me that you'll be leaving tonight to avoid trouble with Sheriff Mintner, I understand. In fact, I hope you do leave for Socorro."

"To hell with Socorro," he said with a frown. "Everyone keeps suggesting I go there, and I don't give a fig for the place. Big Pine suits me right down to the ground."

"For you, Socorro would be healthier."

"Maybe," Clint agreed, "but I intend to use my winnings to set up shop tomorrow morning."

"In the street?"

"Nope. I saw a couple of small buildings that have posted for rent signs on 'em. Guess that's what I'll do."

"Not if the sheriff doesn't approve of it—and he won't."

Clint sighed. He was getting mighty tired of people telling him what the sheriff would or would not permit in Big Pine. And so far, he'd not had the least bit of success trying to make folks understand that every citizen of the United States of America was allowed certain basic rights. Like the right to speak out publically against corruption of office or the right to engage in honest enterprise.

"Sarah," Clint said as patiently as he could, "I told you already that I don't worry too much about Sheriff Mintner. I'm not looking for trouble with the man, but I will not be run out of this town or denied the right to make an honest living if Big Pine is where I choose to do so."

"Lofty but dangerous words," she said. "Why don't we just enjoy tonight and let tomorrow take care of itself?"

He slipped his arm around her waist. It wasn't small like it had probably been when Sarah was twenty, but it was small enough, and when they passed a lamp, Clint looked down at the woman and thought the lamplight was very becoming to her appearance. He also liked the way she slipped her arm around his waist and walked in step with him, trying to match his long strides.

When they arrived at Sarah's shack, Clint could see that the waitress hadn't been modest about her circumstances. The shack looked as if it might once have been a horse barn. It was located behind a larger house, and the holes in the walls were covered with tar paper. It was humble, to say the least.

Inside, however, Clint was pleased to see that the two-room shack was clean and tidy. Sarah had used newspapers to cover the board walls, and her furniture was old and probably secondhand but in good repair. There was a tin stove and a counter where she could wash dishes and things. Several flyspecked old prints glistened in the flickering light of the kerosene lamp that Sarah held up to show him the layout.

"It's real poor," she said. "I know that, and it shames me to bring company, but I keep it clean, and I don't let very many men come here, no matter that you probably think I bring strangers like you home every night."

"I never thought that," Clint said, taking the lamp from her hands and setting it on a crude table. "I feel privileged to be here with you tonight. You know, my room at the Helldorado Hotel isn't exactly a palace."

Sarah smiled. "I'm sure that's true. I've never been in that hotel, it's enough just to walk past the open door of the lobby and smell the stench."

"Well," Clint said, "we're going to change that and . . ."

Sarah wasn't listening. She lifted on her toes and kissed him into silence, and the next thing Clint knew, she was digging at his belt, unbuckling his gun, and then his pants.

"You're in a mighty big hurry, aren't you, darlin'?"

"I'm past thirty years old and I'm running out of time," she told him as he unbuttoned her blouse and then her upper undergarment to reveal her large if somewhat sagging breasts.

When Clint's tongue found her big, dark nipples, Sarah gasped with pleasure and her hands found his manhood. For several minutes, they just swayed together, each arousing the other with their touch.

It was Sarah whose composure broke first. She shucked off her dress and dragged the Gunsmith back to her bed. "Let's stop playing around and get right down to business," she told him as she took him in her mouth.

"Suits me," he breathed, running his hands through the waitress's long hair and feeling her do wondrous things with her lips, mouth, and darting tongue.

"Mmmm," she moaned.

"My oh my," he breathed, rocking back and forth on the balls of his feet and arching his back. "Whatever you're doing, don't stop."

Sarah didn't stop. For several minutes, she teased and sucked and played with his distended manhood until Clint felt as if the top of his head was going to explode.

"I think you're ready for me now," Sarah told the Gunsmith when he was starting to groan with mounting passion. "In fact, you might be too damned ready."

Clint stumbled back, burning with desire. He shucked off his boots and stepped out of his pants. He watched as she positioned herself in the center of her narrow bed, and then he eagerly climbed on top of her. Sarah squealed like a schoolgirl and bucked like a filly.

"I knew the first time I laid eyes on you this evening that you'd be a stud worth getting bred by. I just knew it."

"You haven't seen anything yet," Clint said, vigorously plunging in and out of the woman. "We're going to have a long, lovin' night, Sarah."

"Good! I don't have to be back at the café until five o'clock tomorrow afternoon. It's my aim to keep you off the streets tomorrow morning so that you and the sheriff don't tangle."

Clint growled with pleasure. "I'm afraid that you'll fail at that, darlin'. I've got to find an office and get started makin' money in the morning."

"Shut up and tend to our business," she urged, eyes closing and breath coming faster.

Clint liked this woman. He liked not only the way she worked to satisfy him in bed, but also appreciated her outspoken honesty. There was no guile in Sarah Taylor. She was only a slightly tarnished woman who was probably afraid of growing old and destitute and was doing her damnedest to try and grab whatever pleasure she could while it was hers for the taking.

Clint wanted to give Sarah a full night of pleasure. All his former weariness fell away, and he gripped her buttocks and made her squeal with pleasure until, finally, he could rein himself in no longer, and they both began to slam together, fingers digging into flesh, bodies stiffening in release.

"Ahhh!" Sarah cried, eyes rolling upward as she lost control.

It took several moments until the Gunsmith could catch his breath, then he tried to roll off the waitress, but Sarah locked him to her with arms and legs. "You're going nowhere," she panted.

"I just meant to . . ."

"Let it shrink out slow," she told him. "Like a little worm slipping out of its hole."

Clint laughed outright. "I never heard it described that way."

"It fits, doesn't it?"

"I guess."

Sarah thrust hard at him with her hips. "Don't worry, I'll soon make it rise like a snake charmer does his pet rattler."

"You're a little crazy, you know that, Sarah?"

"Are you complaining?"

"Oh no," he assured her. "Fact is, you're as much of a woman as any healthy man could handle."

Sarah liked that. They were silent for a while, half dozing. Clint was just starting to dream when Sarah poked him in the ribs and said, "How soon can I call up your rattler?"

"Oh, I don't know," he said sleepily.

Sarah rolled him off of her and fell upon his manhood. Watching her in the lamplight, Clint knew damn good and well that his big rattler was about to dance to her sweet music.

Clint awoke just after daybreak. He rolled out of bed and quietly dressed. Even though his night's sleep had been interrupted many times by Sarah Taylor, Clint felt refreshed in mind and spirit. He finished dressing and strapped on his six-gun, then clamped his battered black Stetson on before he laid another five dollars on Sarah's table. He was crazy to leave her with so much, but Sarah was having a hard time making ends meet. Furthermore,

Clint especially appreciated the way that she never asked or expected money from him even though he now had a pocketful of spending cash.

"Things will get better for us both," was Clint's whispered promise as he slipped out the door and stepped into the bright New Mexico sunshine.

First he went over to the livery to see Duke. The black gelding had been curried to a shine and was happily munching on a big bait of oats.

Dan Hurley was cleaning stalls with his grandfather. When he saw the Gunsmith, he came over to say, "I sure like that big, black horse of yours, Mr. Adams. Don't suppose you might be interested in selling or trading for him. My grandpa and I know you're real short of cash, and we was thinkin' that . . ."

"Whoa up there, young fella," Clint said, digging into his pockets and pulling out a roll of cash. "I got a little lucky last night at the Cowboy Saloon, and I'm no longer busted."

The boy's face dropped. "I guess that means you wouldn't be interested in selling Duke, huh?"

"I wouldn't have even if I were dead broke this morning. But if I ever did sell that horse, I'd sell him to you and your grandpa 'cause I know he'd get a good home."

This compliment lifted the boy's spirits. "How'd you win at poker? Every game in Big Pine is fixed one way or the other, so my grandpa says."

"Well," Clint told the boy, "it's a long story, and I'm in need of breakfast and some strong black coffee. You want some breakfast, on me?"

"Why sure!" Dan exclaimed, but then cast a look back over his shoulder. "I'll have to get permission from Gramps, first. There's still some stalls to muck out although they can wait an hour."

"Invite him to join us," Clint said.

"You'd buy us *both* breakfast?"

"What can it cost? Two bits each?"

"Yeah."

"I can handle that," Clint said. "Besides, now that I'm about to become the town's new gunsmith, I consider this a sound promotional expense. And if I make friends and do good work, my business will prosper."

"But I don't even own a gun yet," Dan admitted. "And all my grandpa owns is an old double-barreled shotgun that misfires half the time and . . ."

"See there? You Hurley men *do* need the services of an expert gunsmith! Now, grab Gramps and let's get some coffee, bacon, and biscuits."

"You bet!" Dan said, sprinting barefoot back into the barn.

A moment later, he came out with Dud Hurley in tow. "You musta won big at poker last night, Mr. Adams, you takin' us to breakfast and all."

"I won all right, and I got a feeling that I'm on a roll right now," Clint told the man. "And when I'm on a roll, I like to share my good fortune with my new friends."

Clint stopped, looked closely at each of them. "You Hurleys are my friends, aren't you?"

"Why sure!" they both echoed.

"Good," Clint said, grabbing each of them by the arm and leading them down the street. "You know this town, take us to the best café."

The Hurleys led Clint to the same café where Sarah worked, and that was fine with the Gunsmith. The new early morning waitress was old, crotchety, and tight-lipped, but Clint didn't mind that either. He figured that one good waitress a night was as much as any man could expect.

"What do you want?" the woman demanded.

"Coffee all around."

"Milk for me," Dan said.

"And bring us your big breakfast. Biscuits and gravy, bacon, sausage, and whatever else it comes with."

"For all three?"

"Yep."

The waitress nodded. "You got it, Gunsmith. A man deserves a good last meal."

Clint's jaw dropped. "Now what the hell is that supposed to mean?"

"It means that you won't eat again," Dud Hurley said. "Not after Sheriff Mintner and his deputies come waltzin' in here to tack your green hide to the wall."

Clint frowned. "Nobody said anything about deputies."

"You didn't ask."

"How many?"

The two Hurleys exchanged somber glances. Finally, the old man said, "Depends on the job. The sheriff is a hard man, but he's no fool. By now he'll know that you're the Gunsmith. I'd guess that, right now, he's probably rounding up three or four good hands with a six-gun."

Clint lost his appetite. Up until this moment, he'd just naturally assumed that a small town like Big Pine wouldn't be able to afford more than one lawman. And maybe it couldn't. If Sheriff Mintner was as prosperous as Sarah believed, it only made good sense that the man would not take any unnecessary risks.

"Uh-oh," Dan whispered. "Look who's coming for breakfast."

Clint glanced out the front window and, sure enough, he saw the big sheriff flanked by three hard cases. There was no time to be indecisive. Dragging two dollars out of his pocket, Clint slammed them down on the table and jumped to his feet.

"What are you doing?" Dan shouted.

"I'm getting out of here. Enjoy your breakfasts on me!"

"You're running!" Dan looked shocked and appalled.

"I'm ducking out the back door, if there is one," Clint said. "And if there isn't, I'm *making* one. But don't worry, I'm not leaving town. It's just that I mean to have a talk with Mintner on *my* terms. Not his."

"Shit, you're running," the old man said, pouring coffee for himself. "Not that I blame you. I'd run too, given these poor odds. But if you'd have clued me in, me and the boy would have had that black gelding saddled up this morning and ready to go."

"I won't be needing him—yet!" Clint called back to the Hurleys as he bulled into the kitchen, spied a back door, and headed for it on the run.

FOUR

It had galled the socks off Clint to have to turn tail and run out the back door instead of brace Sheriff Al Mintner. As he'd sprinted out of the café, he'd looked back and seen the expression of disappointment on young Dan Hurley's face, and that had further burned the Gunsmith's pride. Had the trouble been strictly between himself, the sheriff, and his three hired guns, Clint might have tried to get the drop on all four. But to brace such long odds with the boy and his grandfather in the line of fire would have been downright irresponsible.

Now, as Clint raced down the alley, he was not really sure where he was heading. He could hear shouts from the street in front of the café, and Clint was pretty sure that the Hurleys were doing all they could to buy him a little extra escape time. When Clint reached the end of the alley, there was nothing before him but the open valley and a few distant ranch houses. He pivoted and ducked back to the main street, then pulled his Stetson low and sauntered toward the Helldorado Hotel. Clint figured he would get his Winchester, saddlebags, and gear, then find a hiding place until he could manage to catch Sheriff Mintner alone and force a one-on-one showdown.

"Hello there!" a very feminine voice said. "Aren't you the Gunsmith?"

Clint turned to see Angie Buttering standing in the doorway of a general dry goods store. For a moment, Clint didn't know what to do. He only had to glance a block down the street to see Sheriff Mintner and his gunmen crowded around the front of the café. The Hurleys were backed up against a hitching post, and the sheriff was obviously haranguing them.

"Mr. Adams?"

Clint took the woman's arm and pulled her into the store. "Yes," he said, "I am the Gunsmith and, unless you want your sheriff to suddenly contract a severe case of lead poisoning, I'd suggest you stop him from bullying that old man and his grandson."

Angie's blue eyes widened, and then she glanced past the Gunsmith to see what all the commotion was about. "What's the trouble?"

"Your boyfriend took an immediate dislike to me yesterday, and it appears that dislike has turned into pure hatred. I'm sure what he intends to do is run me out of town on a rail—or worse."

"Then why don't you leave Big Pine?"

"Because I've got a right to go where the hell I want to go and stay as long as I want, providing I don't break the law—which I haven't."

Clint glared at the pretty woman. "What is wrong with you people, anyway? What kind of town is this that allows a sheriff to harass newcomers and probably extort protection money from its merchants?"

Angie's cheeks burned red. "Now listen here, Mr. Adams! We don't pay any extortion or *protection* money to Sheriff Mintner."

"Well, then, I'll bet you're one of the few who don't," Clint said hotly. "And what about the way that your sheriff is bullying that old man and boy right now?"

Angie shook with anger, but when she said nothing, Clint pushed out of the doorway and started down the boardwalk fully intending to force a showdown, long odds be damned.

"Wait!" she cried, catching his sleeve and pulling him around. "I'll . . . I'll stop it!"

Clint hesitated. He still hadn't been seen by the sheriff or his deputies and was of the opinion that a gun battle in the middle of town was the worst possible way to settle his differences with a corrupt town sheriff. More than once in his law career, he'd seen innocent bystanders killed by stray bullets, and that was something the Gunsmith had no wish to have repeated in Big Pine.

"All right," he conceded. "You go down there and whip that boyfriend of yours into line. If you don't, I swear I'll put a bullet in his gizzard before his gunnies can down me."

Angie Buttering's eyebrows raised. "Are you trying to tell me that you'd actually go down there and get yourself killed rather than let Allen give the Hurleys nothing more than a tongue-lashing?"

"I'm not a bluffer."

Angie took a long look at Clint and seemed to finally realize that he wasn't bluffing. And that, if she did not intervene, the Gunsmith really was going to kill her sheriff.

"All right. I'll put a stop to it," she said. "But first you have to promise not to kill Allen. Not that I'm convinced that you even could."

"I won't promise anything," Clint snapped. "If the man is fool enough to draw on me or try to put me in jail, I'll do what's necessary."

"What is necessary is for you to *leave town*!"

"No," Clint countered, "it's for you to get down there and get your boyfriend to leave that old man and his grandson alone before I put a permanent plug in Mintner's gizzard."

Angie shivered with hatred. "You're a damn stubborn fool! I hate you!"

"Are you going down there, or am I?" Clint growled.

"I'll go." She grabbed his sleeve and pushed him back toward the general store. "Go inside and wait. Don't you dare come out looking for more trouble."

"Hell, Miss Buttering," Clint said, "neither you nor your boyfriend know what real trouble is until you see me get upset."

Angie started to say something but thought better of it. "Humph!" she snorted, then marched down the board-walk.

Clint took a deep breath and let it out slowly. Then, because he'd given the woman his word, he went into the general store, stabbed a pickle out of a barrel, and bit it in half.

"Damn woman!" he swore. "She's as bad as the sheriff when you get right down to it."

"Are you talking about my daughter?" a gentle voice inquired.

Clint twisted around to see a frail man in his fifties standing in one of the aisles. "She's your daughter?"

"That's right." The man had been stocking a shelf and was wearing an apron. He looked sickly, and when he stepped toward the Gunsmith, he turned so that Clint could see that he was missing both his right arm and leg. In the latter case, he was wearing a wooden stump under his trousers that banged on the floorboards.

"Mr. Buttering," Clint said, at once feeling guilty for

his words, "I'm sure that your daughter is a fine girl. Just a little headstrong. That's all I meant, really."

"My name is Bill Buttering," the man said, extending his left hand. "I know Angie is headstrong and, if it helps us understand one another any better, I also disapprove of Sheriff Mintner."

"Listen," Clint said awkwardly, "forget what I said just now. It's just that Mintner and I have gotten off to a bad start."

"Yes, so I've heard. When Angie told me that you were in town, I knew that there would be trouble."

"How'd you know that?" Clint asked with puzzlement. "I sure never expected trouble. I came looking to rest myself and my horse. Maybe spend the summer here working as a gunsmith."

"I know. Dud Hurley came in and told me about your plans. He and I are good friends and old confidants, so please don't think Dud is going all around Big Pine telling everyone your business."

"Never entered my mind."

"Well," Buttering said, "we both agreed that Sheriff Mintner wouldn't allow a famous lawman to settle in Big Pine, much less open up a competing gunsmith business."

"Well, that's just what I aim to do, sheriff or no sheriff," Clint declared.

"Why don't you just ride away from all this?" Buttering said quietly. "We've got a bad problem here, but someday, we'll get it solved by ourselves."

"Is that right?" Clint challenged. "And how will that happen? The sheriff has this town locked up tighter than a Wells Fargo strongbox. He has the money and the badge, and he's got at least three hired guns backing up his play.

How do you or anyone else in Big Pine intend to rein in Sheriff Mintner?"

Buttering tried to form a good answer, but failed. "I . . . I'll shoot him myself," he stammered. "Look at me! What do I have to live for except my daughter?"

"Listen," Clint said after a long pause, "it's clear that you've already fought your share of battles. Which side were you on, the Union or the Confederacy?"

"Confederacy."

Clint knew that there were still quite a few of these shot-to-pieces old Civil War veterans scattered about the West. And while Bill Buttering had somehow survived two major amputations, it was clear that they'd broken his health and shortened his life span.

"I could ambush him. That's what I'll do! I'll just wait until he steps into this store, and I'll shoot him before he knows what is going to happen."

"Bad idea."

"Better *I* kill him than you! I should have done it years ago. I should have done it the first time he came by to court my daughter!"

The Gunsmith could see that Buttering was serious and very, very desperate. "Tell you what," Clint said, "why don't you let me see if there's a better way to work this out? I might be able to come up with something that would keep you from prison, or worse."

"Like what, for instance?"

"I don't know yet," Clint confessed. "Right now, I'm on the dodge, and I'm just buying a little time before I can figure out how to get the drop on Mintner and try to teach him a few lessons about the law."

"He won't listen!" Buttering took a hobbling stop forward. "Allen Mintner is a *killer*! He's greedy and treacherous. I know you're probably faster with a gun than he is, but you won't be able to catch him without his so-called deputies crowded around to protect him. And sooner or later, he'll find you in this town. It's too small to hide in for very long."

Clint knew that things did look bleak, but as long as there was life, there was hope. "Just give me a few days," he urged. "Don't tell your daughter about this conversation. Let's just keep our opinion of Sheriff Mintner to ourselves. Just give me a little time to work things out."

"Where can you hide that is safe?"

"I may saddle my horse and head for the hills."

"He'll turn this town upside down looking for you."

"To hell with him."

He went over to the door and peered up the street. True to her promise, Angie had intervened, and the Hurleys were walking back toward their livery. It was plain to see that Sheriff Mintner was furious, and it was all that Angie could do to keep him under control.

"What does she see in that man besides power and money?" Clint mused aloud.

"I don't know," the storekeeper said with desolation corroding his voice. "I've asked my daughter that very same question a hundred times. I'm just glad that her dear mother isn't still alive to see what's become of Angie." He shook his head, looking confused and beaten. "I can't imagine what she is thinking."

Clint's guess was that Sarah Taylor had pegged Angie correctly when she'd said that Angie was attracted to the promise of money and position. Mintner was in line to become extremely wealthy during the next few years, and one day he'd be the mayor, the banker, the judge and the jury in Big Pine. As Mrs. Mintner, Angie would be assured of her own place at the head of the social line, and she'd wield enough power and influence to sit at the top of Big Pine's social pecking order.

Well, Clint thought, I'm going to throw a limb in Mintner's spokes and see if I can't turn his wagon load of ambitions upside down.

"What are you going to do now?" Buttering asked as Clint stepped back into the store.

"You have a back door, don't you?"

"Yes."

"Then that's where I'm going," the Gunsmith replied. "And remember your promise not to murder the sheriff. When the dust settles, I got a strong feeling that your daughter is going to need her father."

Buttering tried to choke back a sob but failed. It was clear that he had reached the end of his emotional tether. Bill Buttering, if Clint was any judge, was a man very near the breaking point.

"It'll work out." Clint shifted awkwardly. "Take heart, sir. Things will get better, I promise."

Buttering tried to smile. "If it doesn't, if the sheriff or one of his deputies kills you, then I'm going to shoot the son of a bitch even if I have to do it in the back through a shelf of tinned goods!"

"If I'm dead, you can rest assured you will have my full support to gun the son of a bitch down any way you can," Clint said as, for the second time in an hour, he sought refuge in a back alley.

Outside, he looked in both directions and decided that it would be too predictable to head for the livery. If Mintner had any brains at all, he'd already have one of his deputies hiding by the Hurley stable close to Duke both night and day.

Clint took a deep breath and considered the other options. It would also be foolish to return to the Helldorado Hotel. That meant that he'd better come up with the last place in Big Pine that the sheriff would expect to find him.

Clint smiled with sudden inspiration. He stepped back into the Buttering's general store and almost bumped into Angie's father and knocked him down.

"Change your mind?" Buttering asked. "I'm sure willing to hide you back here in the storeroom."

"I've got a better idea," Clint said, deciding that he could trust this man with his life. "Where does the sheriff live?"

"One block over on . . . say, you aren't . . ."

"Yep. I'm going to beard the lion in his own den," Clint announced. "So give me directions, and I'll be on my way."

Buttering stared at him with disbelief, and then he finally smiled. "Well, I'll be damned! That *is* the very last place the sheriff would think to look!"

"Where is it and how can I get there with the least bit of attention?"

Buttering pursed his lips, then his eyes brightened. "Did you see that buckboard in the alley?"

"I think so."

"Well, I've got a man coming in pretty quick to load it with supplies. Supplies that are to be delivered to Mintner's next-door neighbor."

"Can your man be trusted?"

"He hates the sheriff almost as much as I do," Buttering said.

"In that case," Clint replied, "I think we have the perfect answer to our problem. You can throw a tarp over me and the supplies. When we get there, your man can tell me when to unload when no one is looking."

"Our delivery is always to the back door. You can hop out in the alley and no one will see you."

"Does the sheriff own a watchdog?"

"Not unless you count the two-legged kind."

"Good," Clint said. "Then let's get that tarp so I can get out of here before your daughter or the sheriff comes waltzing in the front door."

"She won't betray you," Buttering said. "Angie wouldn't do that."

Clint dipped his chin in agreement, but he didn't believe it. And though he'd never tell poor Bill Buttering his feelings, he wouldn't have trusted Angie as far as he could throw the scheming, ruthless, little gold digger.

FIVE

"All right," Bill Buttering said, "roll 'em, and don't look back over your shoulder, Clem. Just drive right up to Mrs. James's house like you always do and . . ."

"Hell, Bill! What do you take me fer?" the driver crabbed. "I'm no durned fool!"

"Not most of the time, anyway," Bill said to his deliveryman.

"Could we just get going?" Clint demanded. "It's hot, and this damn tarp smells like it's been used to cover chicken shit!"

"That's because it has," Bill replied, "but there's no time to go into that now."

Clint was about to crawl out from under the tarp and figure a better way to reach the sheriff's house when the wagon jerked forward and they were finally under way. He was sprawled across the bed of the buckboard between bags of flour and other dry goods. This was a hell of a way to go about things, but a man had to do what was necessary when he was being hunted like a coon by a pack of hound dogs.

"How you doin' back there, Gunsmith?" Clem asked.

"Shhh! For cripes sake!"

"Aw, nobody listens to old Clem anyway. Mostly, I just talk and then listen to myself. Sometimes I say the damnedest things, too! Smart, that's what they don't realize I am."

"Fine," Clint hissed, "but would you just shut up and deliver me!"

"Sure thing, Mr. Gunsmith. But you should see the expression on Sheriff Mintner's face! He's standing outside his office and looks like a teased polecat, ready to scratch and spit. I'd say he wants you right bad."

"And he'll have me, too, if you don't shut up!"

"Well, sir, no one lives forever. Now that's wisdom comin' straight from the heart of old Clem. It's a wisdom that you can't argue with no matter if you can read, write, or whatever."

The Gunsmith just groaned and hoped that the prattling old fool would not ruin everything. The minutes passed slowly, and then finally the wagon stopped. Clint started to wiggle out from under the tarp, but Clem's words stopped him.

"Afternoon, Mr. Evans! How's the bankin' business today?"

"Same as I told you yesterday, Clem. Slow but profitable. You still planning to open a little account with us?"

"Might be I will, if I can do 'er with fifty cents."

"I'm afraid that five dollars is our minimum," Evans said. "Can't you get Mr. Buttering to give you a small advance on your salary? Your five dollars could be earning interest right this very minute as we talk. The current rate is three percent."

"What does that mean?"

"It means that your five dollars will earn fifteen cents a year!"

"Fifteen cents!" Clem sounded outraged. "Fer a whole damn year!"

"Well . . . yes."

"That's the poorest damn deal I ever heard of, Mr. Evans. Damned if I'd wait a whole year to spend my five dollars just so I could earn a lousy fifteen cents, the price of three damned cigars."

Even under the tarp, Clint could hear the disgust and anger in the banker's voice. "Well then, Clem, I'd suggest you just forget about opening a bank account. Go ahead and squander your future. Save nothing for old age."

"I already done that!"

"If you'd have opened an account when you were a boy, you'd have lots of money right now instead of living hand-to-mouth."

"Shoot, Mr. Evans, there weren't no banks when I was a young man! Wasn't even a *town* of Big Pine back then, you durned stuff-shirt fool!"

"You're impossible," Evans snorted, and Clint heard the banker's boots marching away.

"Damned fool," Clem groused to himself.

"*You're* the fool!" Clint hissed from under the tarp. "And so help me God, if you stop and go into some long-winded conversation like that again while I'm under here dying for fresh air, I'll put a bullet up your backside so you'll have *two* assholes!"

Clint heard the crack of a buggy whip, and the wagon jerked forward so violently he slid backward across the buckboard's floor and had to pull his boots back under the tarp. After what seemed like an hour but was probably only a few minutes, the buckboard stopped, and Clint heard Clem set the brake and felt the springs sway as the driver climbed down.

"Afternoon, Mrs. James!" Clem called. "Nice to see you up and around this fine day."

"I'm always up and around, you blathering old fool!" the lady replied. "And it's about time that you finally got here with my supplies. I'm baking today, and I haven't got any flour. What took you so long? The delivery was supposed to be here first thing in the morning!"

"Well, ma'am, sometimes we aren't always on schedule in Big Pine. You ought to know that by now."

"You're *never* on schedule! Now let's unload that wagon so I can get to baking!"

Clint drew in his breath and held it, sure that the old woman was going to see him under the tarp and let out a scream. But then he heard Clem say, "You got to pay me in advance today, Mrs. James. Boss says that you're a little behind and you need to catch up on your bill."

"What?"

"Sorry, ma'am. But before I unload so much as a pound of goods, I've got to see some cash money."

"This is outrageous! My bill is paid up in full, and you know that as well as Mr. Buttering!"

"Sorry, ma'am. Just following orders. No money, no delivery. It's as simple as that."

"Damn you, you stupid old coot! Mr. Buttering will hear about this insulting behavior!"

"Does that mean you've got the cash?"

"I'll get it, and then I'll give Mr. Buttering a piece of my mind!"

"Thank you, ma'am."

Clint heard the back door slam, and then Clem whispered, "All right, Gunsmith, the coast is clear. Get out and clear out before that old battle-ax returns."

Clint didn't need any urging. He crawled out, sucked in a breath of fresh air, and then jumped to the ground smelling awful. "I'm sure not happy about the way this worked out either," he growled. "Which is Sheriff Mintner's house?"

"That one," Clem said, pointing. "Best get out of here now, Gunsmith, before Mrs. James comes back, or things could get real interesting."

"I'm afraid they already will be for poor Mr. Buttering," Clint said as he hopped over a low picket fence into the sheriff's yard, then ducked under his porch as the James woman crashed outside to give Clem money and a good piece of her mind.

Despite smelling like a henhouse, Clint had to grin as he listened to the old woman give Clem hell. She was hopping mad, and Clem was getting red-faced as well trying to hold his own temper. Finally, Clem's temper broke, and he grabbed a sack of flour and threw it at the back of the house. The sack exploded like a huge desert cloud of alkali dust. The old lady went crazy and tried to grab Clem's buggy whip and use it on him.

For several minutes, the pair struggled over the whip, and it was a real question as to who would win the contest. Finally, Clem overcame Mrs. James, and the battle was over. A few minutes later, the wagon was unloaded, and both old people were riding stiff-backed back into town. The Gunsmith knew that poor Mr. Buttering was going to be in for a rough time when his delivery wagon reappeared.

The Gunsmith waited until no one was in sight, then he climbed out from under the porch, drew his six-gun, and tiptoed into the house, closing the back door behind him. He was in the kitchen and moved quickly into the hallway. Without making a sound, he tiptoed through the hallway, then turned right and went upstairs.

There were three bedrooms, and all of them were empty. Clint chose to spend time waiting in the sheriff's own bedroom. He found a bucket and fancy copper bathtub. He decided to use the latter right away and went downstairs to pump water.

After a shave and bath, he found a nice suit of clothes to replace his own that smelled so bad. Mintner's suit was long enough in the pants legs and sleeves, but a little baggy about the waist. Sheriff Mintner was carrying about thirty extra pounds of fat but, otherwise, his clothes were a reasonably good fit and of the highest quality. It was plain to see that the man had expensive tastes. Clint even found a nice pair of boots that were exactly his own size and his favorite boot color—black.

Unfortunately, their hat sizes were different, the sheriff's being a half-size larger. No matter, the sheriff's cigars were first-rate and so was his brandy. Clint reclined in a rocking chair beside Mintner's upstairs bedroom window. It was a pleasant day, and Clint was inclined to take his ease and wait for Sheriff Mintner as long as it took. He smoked, rocked, sipped, and smoked some more looking down through a mulberry tree at the yard and the passersby.

Clint must have dozed in the rocking chair, because when he awoke, it was to hear the heavy pounding of boots coming up the stairs. Half-asleep, Clint rolled out of the rocking chair and dove behind the bed just as the door swung open and Sheriff Mintner stomped in, puffing on his own cigar.

The sheriff paused at the door and called back down the stairs. "You tell the boys I'll meet them at the Chuck Wagon Café in thirty minutes, and we'll get something to eat before we finish tearing this town apart! We'll find the Gunsmith, by Gawd, or I'll know the reason why!"

"Maybe he rode off already."

"Without that big, black horse, his Winchester rifle, and saddlebags?" the sheriff hollered. "I damn sure don't think so!"

Clint lifted his head above the level of the bed and saw the sheriff slam the door shut and then turn. Clint let the man march over to the bed and collapse upon it, cigar still clenched between his teeth.

"Son of a bitch!" Sheriff Mintner cursed. "Damn!"

Clint smiled, knowing he was the source of the sheriff's consternation. He drew his gun and stood up in one fluid motion, saying, "Life can be a real bitch some days, can't it, Sheriff?"

Mintner was so shocked that he opened his mouth to yell and the cigar dropped down his gullet, almost choking him. He gagged, batted burning ashes across himself and the bed, then began to dig the cigar out of his throat. Finally succeeding, he yelped with pain as the cigar burned a hole through his vest and put a blister on his chest.

"Easy," Clint said, picking up the cigar and dropping it onto an expensive rug before he ground it under his new boot heel. "One shout and I'll put a bullet through that blister, and it'll hurt a lot worse, I'll guarantee you."

Mintner's eyes bulged with fear. Still choking and red-faced, his eyes focused on the six-gun in Clint's fist.

"What the hell are you doing here?" he wheezed. "And . . . you're wearing my suit!"

"Keep your voice down," Clint ordered. He lifted one leg. "And thanks for the boots. Mine were worn down to nothing and these are a perfect fit."

"You son of a bitch!" the lawman snarled.

"Don't rile me," Clint said, waving his Colt.

"You gonna kill me?" Mintner breathed.

"Probably not. What I *am* going to do is find out why you're so set against my opening a little gunsmithing business in Big Pine. Seems to me that you're doing so well you shouldn't mind the competition. Hell, you're the sheriff of this town, not the owner. From what I hear, you've got your hands into about every pocket there is in these parts."

"Not true! I'm just an underpaid officer of the law, like you used to be! You know that we never make what we're worth."

Clint looked around at the expensive furnishings and plucked another expensive cigar from Mintner's coat. "Seems to me that you're doing exceptionally well, Sheriff."

Mintner gulped. "Listen, if you want to make some money, I'll hire you to be one of my deputies."

"*Deputies?* Is that what you call those gunnies that were flanking you down in the street? Where I come from, that kind are either arrested, run out of town, or hanged on general principle."

"Look," Mintner breathed, "I know that you think I was trying to arrest you."

"That's right."

"But I was just putting on a show for the people. There's an election coming up, and I wanted them to see that I wasn't afraid of a man with a reputation. I'd have turned you loose and given you a few bucks if you'd asked."

"What a fine fellow you are," Clint said. "But I'd rather make up my own mind about where I go and when I go. It's a free country, Sheriff. Or haven't you heard?"

"Listen," Mintner said, "how about I give you a hundred dollars and we both shake hands and then you ride?"

"Nothing doing. I'm going to open a business and see that you start sticking to sheriffing. Is that understood? And if you or any of your gunnies interfere, I'll make sure that you won't even be around to campaign for sheriff during this upcoming election. Is *that* understood?"

Beads of sweat were running down the sheriff's face. He nodded vigorously. "Sure, I just overreacted, that's all."

"Sure," Clint said, holstering his gun. He grabbed the sheriff by the shirtfront and yanked the man to his feet. "Why don't you take me out to dinner and tell your *deputies* that we're friends now?"

"Why, of course!"

Clint propelled the man toward the door. Right now, he had Sheriff Mintner so spooked he would say or do anything. But later, when the man was surrounded by his gunnies, it might just be an entirely different story.

Only time would tell. But until then, at least Clint was going to be Big Pine's new well-fed, well-dressed gunsmith.

SIX

Dinner with Sheriff Mintner and his three deputies was neither cordial nor relaxing, but Clint ordered the biggest steak on the menu with mashed potatoes, gravy, and carrots, topped off with apple pie and coffee for dessert.

"The thing of it is," he said straight-faced to his grim dining companions, "I am a damned fine gunsmith, and I'd appreciate your business."

The sheriff blanched. "You threaten to kill me and my men, then you have the gall to ask for our patronage?"

"Why not?" Clint shrugged. "I'm not one to hold onto hard feelings. The way I see it, Al, you and your boys just overstepped your bounds. But now, since this meal is on your tab, I figure it's as good as an apology, and I'm willing to let bygones be bygones."

"That's real friendly of you," one of the sheriff's deputies said. "But you're blowin' nothing but smoke. And while I don't understand what we're doin' settin' around the table with someone like you when we should be rawhidin' you out of town on a rail, I . . ."

"What's your name?" Clint asked the tough-looking man sitting across from him.

"Why . . . Jed Cotton, but what the hell has . . ."

49

"Jed, would you like a refill on your coffee? I noticed you were out."

Cotton frowned, glanced at the sheriff, who shrugged his shoulders to indicate he also hadn't a clue as to what direction the Gunsmith was headed.

"Waitress!" Clint called. "Could you bring a fresh pot of coffee over here for Deputy Jed Cotton?"

"Sure."

When the waitress came, Clint intercepted her and took the steaming pot of coffee. Then, he stepped over to Cotton's side and poured it into his cup and just kept pouring . . . and pouring . . . and pouring.

"Hey! What the hell are you—hey!"

The coffee overflowed and spilled onto Cotton's pants. He howled and jumped back, almost upsetting the table. Cotton was so incensed that he clawed for his gun. Without seeming to hurry, Clint smashed the man in the face with the nearly empty coffeepot. Cotton crashed over an empty table. The man was in pain and so completely unnerved that he scrambled for the front door, and Clint let him go without additional damages.

Clint looked at the sheriff and his other deputies. With a good-natured grin, he said, "You boys ever notice how bad accidents happen to those that say hard things?"

No one said a word.

"Well, I have," Clint continued with a frown. "And I sure hope none of the rest of you start having bad accidents because of hard talk."

The sheriff flushed with anger. "You run a strong bluff, Adams. But there's still three of us and, like you said, accidents *can* happen."

"Yeah," Clint said, "they sure can. And I'm thinking you might be overdue for one if you're not real careful, Sheriff."

"We'll see," Mintner gritted.

"I'll be opening up for business tomorrow morning."

"I don't think your business is goin' to flourish in Big Pine," another of the deputies snarled. "And I don't think you'll find anyone dumb enough to rent you a shop. You'll have to set up a table in the street and that sure ain't goin' to impress anybody."

Clint rose to his feet. "There are several shops that I've noticed for sale or for rent. I don't expect I'll have any trouble coming to terms with someone. However, if I hear that you boys have been saying bad things about me, then I might just have to ask you to join me for another cup of coffee. *Comprende?*"

The sheriff and his men didn't nod, but they understood Clint's meaning. He left them looking as if they could kill him with their eyes. When Clint stepped out in the street, he drew another of Sheriff Mintner's excellent cigars from his new suit pocket and bit it off. Lighting the cigar, he went for a stroll up and down the boardwalk, taking note of the few empty shops and peering inside, trying to decide which one would best suit his purposes.

It was after ten o'clock when the Gunsmith retired to his room at the Helldorado Hotel. He'd seen Sarah Taylor cleaning up at the café and had a strong urge to walk her home and repeat last night's pleasures, but he was dog-tired and in need of a full night's sleep.

As he entered the lobby, Clint nodded to the clerk, gave the place a quick inspection, and said, "Looking pretty good tonight, Ernie. Where are Horse and Hank this evening?"

"They checked out last night after you beat the hell outta them."

"Sorry about that," Clint said. "But I think that they

were not the kind of guests that you should be attracting. With a clean lobby and a little spit and polish, you can do much better in this hotel. Just keep the cuspidors clean and out where the spitters can see them, and keep the drunks outside. You follow me?"

"Sure I do," the clerk said. "I've been telling the owner that for the last year. But Sheriff Mintner says that—"

"The sheriff owns this hotel?"

"Yes, sir! The former owner had a sudden emergency and left town in a hurry. I guess he probably had to sell this place real cheap."

"Yeah," Clint mused, "I'm sure that Sheriff Mintner made a whale of a good deal. Good night, Ernie."

"Good night," the clerk called.

When Clint reached his room, he saw the edge of a note that had been slipped under his door. He retrieved it and realized at once that it was from Miss Angie Buttering, though the note was unsigned.

Dear Mr. Adams: I am very concerned about your situation and the way that my father was used by you to further your own means. I would like to meet with me privately tomorrow. It is very important that this meeting take place without the sheriff's knowledge. Please find a way to let me know if this is acceptable.

Clint frowned. He didn't like the way that Angie said that he had used her father to further his own means. Hadn't the girl even the slightest clue that her father hated the sheriff? Could she really be so obsessed with marrying wealth and power that she would sell her soul to wed such a hard and unscrupulous man? Clint was still asking himself those questions when he drifted off to sleep.

• • •

The Gunsmith arose refreshed and eager to shave, dress, and venture out for an early breakfast. By nine o'clock he was knocking on doors and inquiring about shop space on Big Pine's main street.

Very quickly, however, Clint learned that the sheriff's deputies had already put out the word that no one was to cooperate with the Gunsmith. By 10:30 that morning, Clint could see that the town was against him, and that he was going to be fighting an uphill battle if he intended to go into business.

It was, to say the least, highly discouraging, and Clint briefly considered the idea of taking everyone's advice and riding on to Socorro. There he could start out fresh and probably have no trouble at all promoting his gunsmithing business.

"Mr. Adams?"

Clint turned to see young Dan Hurley. The boy wore a serious expression when he said, "It's not going too good, is it?"

"Nope," Clint admitted. "It's not. It seems that I'm running out of options."

"You could set up a table under an awning or tree or something. Or maybe my grandpa would lend you a stall to work in where you could put up a . . ."

"Hold up!" Clint said with a laugh. "I can't work in a barn or a blacksmith shop."

"But why not?"

"I have to have good light, and my working space has to be almost dust-free. Dust and dirt in the air can gum up the springs of a six-shooter, and that's often why they quit working. Now, I appreciate your idea, and I'm downright flattered by your offer, but it just won't do."

"Then what *are* you going to do?"

"I'm not sure," Clint admitted. "I would guess that, by now, everyone in Big Pine understands the rules of this game I'm playing against Sheriff Mintner. And if they really want some changes here, they'd better step forward and help me get a foothold in this town. Otherwise, I might just have to check Duke out of his stall and ride on."

"I sure hope you don't have to do that, Mr. Adams."

"Me, too, but I will if I have to."

Clint was about to continue when a movement caught the corner of his eye. He looked down the street and recognized Bill Buttering standing in front of his general store. The Civil War veteran was waving his one arm, motioning for Clint to come visit.

"I wonder what Mr. Buttering wants with you?" Dan said.

"Only one way to find out."

Clint placed a hand on the boy's shoulder. It was his experience that children were often the very best judges of character. Far better than adults. Maybe it was because people didn't often try to con children because there was so little that they yet had to offer.

"What do you think of Mr. Buttering?" Clint asked.

"He's a damned fine man and a real straight shooter," the boy said without hesitation. "He's my grandpa's best friend, and that's good enough for me."

"Me, too," Clint agreed.

He gave Dan a nickel and said, "Brush up Duke and have him ready, just in case I have to move along and find a new place to settle."

Dan studied the nickel and didn't look very happy. "I sure hope that won't be the case," he said before he turned and walked back to his family's livery.

Clint watched the ragged, towheaded boy with more than a little affection. He had a feeling that young Dan would someday turn out to be a real fine man.

The Gunsmith headed down the street to see what Bill Buttering wanted. Maybe it was to set up a meeting with his daughter, though Clint didn't expect that to be the case.

"Good morning," Buttering said in greeting.

"Morning." Clint cocked back his Stetson and waited to see what was on the man's mind.

"The news is all over town that you had Sheriff Mintner right under your thumb and that you poured boiling coffee over Jed Cotton and lived to walk away."

"Cotton was pretty angry. I expect I'll have to watch out for my backside. But right now, I'm running into a stone wall. Might have to leave Big Pine if I don't find a shop to ply my trade."

"That's what I wanted to speak to you about," Buttering said. "I just happen to own a little store. It's been shuttered for almost two years, and it's cramped, dusty, and in real rough shape, but it might work for you."

"You talking about that little boarded-up hole-in-the-wall next door to your general store?" Clint asked, jerking his thumb toward a boarded-up shop.

"Yep."

Clint scowled. He'd not even considered the boarded-up place because it looked so small and rough. Even the front door seemed extra slim, and there was only one window in the front and it was shattered.

"Listen," Buttering said, "I know it's a mess, but if you swept it out, fixed it up, gave it a coat of paint, and fixed the door and the window, I'd give you the first month's rent free."

"You would?"

"Sure! And we'd be neighbors and could kind of watch out for each other, if you know what I mean."

Clint knew exactly what the one-armed, one-legged merchant meant. "You sure you want to buy into this kind of trouble, Bill?"

"I'm sure."

"What about your daughter?" Clint toed the ground with his new boot. "Have you talked this over with her yet? I can't imagine she'd want you to risk your life trying to give me a hand. After all, Sheriff Mintner is paramount in her future plans."

"Angie is making the biggest mistake of her life," Bill said hotly. "And no, I haven't discussed this with her. I own my store and the little shop I'm willing to let you open. Someday Angie will inherit both places, but not until after I'm gone. And until then, I decide how to handle things."

Clint took a deep breath. For an instant, he considered telling the man about his daughter's note, then rejected the idea. Better, he thought, if he just met with Angie and learned firsthand what was on her mind. She was probably going to be furious if he accepted her father's offer of the small shop next door. But Bill was right, this was not his daughter's decision.

"Let's take a look at the place," Clint said. "You got a key to the front door?"

"Naw, better to just rip off those boards on the front and walk inside. I got a hammer in my store. I'll get it for you."

"Okay," Clint said, deciding that maybe he would stay in Big Pine and play this hand out to the end. The truth was, if Bill Buttering was willing to risk his own bacon to give Clint a chance, then that chance ought to be taken.

"Here we go," Buttering said a few minutes later. "A brand-new hammer and crowbar. And if you decide to open the place and fix her up, I'll pay for all the paint, nails, and whatever else you need to do the job."

"You sure are being generous."

"Well," Bill said, "as you can probably guess, I haven't got that much to lose. If you fix it up and then get yourself shot, maybe I can rent it out again."

"Thanks for the vote of confidence," Clint said drily.

Bill Buttering barked a laugh that didn't work. He frowned and said, "There's another thing I think you ought to know."

"And that is?"

"I'm hoping that you kill Sheriff Mintner so he can't snare my Angie into marriage. Hell, maybe she'll even take a shine to *you!*"

"Stranger things have happened," Clint said, wondering if he'd been insulted.

"Nothing would suit me better," Buttering admitted. "Why, if you were of a mind to settle down permanent, someday you could inherit my business and . . ."

"Whoa!" Clint said with a laugh. "We're getting way ahead of ourselves, aren't we?"

The man blushed. "Yeah," he confessed. "I guess so. But I'm also a little desperate. Until you came to Big Pine, I'd been about ready to take a gun and shoot Mintner myself before he totally corrupted my daughter. I'm hopin' you'll save me the trouble."

Clint nodded. He knew that this old, crippled man was just being honest. "We'll see," he said. "We'll just play the game out and see what happens."

SEVEN

Sarah Taylor stood in front of the little store with an amused look on her face and her hands resting on her shapely hips. She watched as Clint struggled to sweep the floor. She heard him cough as big clouds of dust roiled up inside, and she finally took mercy on the Gunsmith and waded through the cloud, taking the broom from his hand.

"You don't beat the dust, you *move* it into a dustpan."

"I don't have one."

"Then go ask Mr. Buttering, and I'm sure that he'll loan you one of his," she said. "I'll finish up with the sweeping."

Clint mopped the sweat from his brow. "I sure appreciate your help, Sarah."

"I just don't want you too tired tonight," she said with a wink.

Clint smiled. "Be right back."

Sarah looked around the little store and was appalled by its sad state of disrepair. Not only was the front window bashed out, but the door was hanging on one hinge, the interior walls were in need of paint, and a counter of some sort was splintered and broken. Even the dust-covered floor was unstable, some boards loose and feeling as if they were rotten.

"It's worse than my shack," she muttered to herself before setting to work with the broom.

She began to hum a tune, and there was a soft smile on her face when she thought about their upcoming night of lovemaking. Sarah had no illusions that she could prevent the Gunsmith from moving on when he tired of either her or Big Pine. Men like Clint Adams were a restless breed, and they generally made terrible husbands, if you could get them to marry at all. But while they belonged to a woman, they were exciting and fun. And that was what Sarah figured she needed for a while.

Until Clint Adams had sat down to eat at the café where she worked, her life had been drudgery. Oh, now and then she would take a liking to a cowboy, and she might even take him to bed. But those relationships were usually just one-night stands, and they never lasted. But with Clint, she had a feeling that she might actually become his woman for a month, perhaps even two. She was going to try her damnedest to help him in any way she could, and when he left, well, perhaps he would even invite her to go along, too.

"So," Sheriff Mintner said, appearing in the doorway, "you and the Gunsmith have gotten to be real cozy, have you, Miss Taylor?"

She felt a shiver pass down her spine and forced herself to keep sweeping.

"I asked you a question!"

Sarah looked up. "I'm sorry," she said as innocently as possible. "What did you say?"

"I said that you and the Gunsmith appear to have gotten off to a very cozy start." Mintner frowned. "How long have you been in Big Pine, Miss Taylor?"

"About . . . a year."

"Do you like it here?"

"What do you mean?"

Mintner shrugged his round shoulders. "I mean, does the town suit you?"

"Yes, it does."

"Now, I know that you live in a shack like a common whore—which you pretty much are—and that don't sit too well in a nice family town."

Sarah clenched the broom handle. "I think you'd better leave me alone, Sheriff. Clint is just next door, and he'll be back any minute."

"Oh, I'm sure he will," the sheriff replied in an acid tone of voice, "but I thought we ought to have a little chat. And I'm afraid that I've come to the conclusion that you are morally unfit to remain in Big Pine."

"You can go straight to hell!"

Minter stepped up and tore the broom handle from her grasp. His face was ugly with spite. "Lady, I do believe you're missing my point. Unless you improve the quality of your company, I'm going to run your cheap ass out of Big Pine. On a stage, or a slab—that's up to you."

Sarah felt her knees weaken while her mouth went dry. She tried to bluster and demand that this man leave at once, but she was so frightened by his threat that she could barely speak. Where was the Gunsmith?

"You think about it," the sheriff said. "Think real hard. And by the way, I understand that a two-bit tip at the café will buy a man a tumble in your bed."

Sarah took a swing at him, but Mintner grabbed her wrist and twisted it until tears sprang to her eyes. "Let go of me!"

He released her wrist and stepped back. "I'll tell my deputies about you, Miss Taylor. One of them might think that you are worth two bits—but don't get your hopes up."

He tipped his hat to her and smiled coldly. "You better mend your ways, Miss Taylor. You better mend them real fast."

As soon as he was gone, Sarah leaned against the overturned counter and struggled to beat down her terror. After a moment, she hurried to the door, almost turned toward the general store to cry on Clint's shoulder, then saw a deputy standing across the street.

"My God," she whispered, "they're watching me!"

Sarah turned around and rushed off down the street.

When Clint returned with the dustpan, he was surprised to see that Sarah had already left. He guessed he shouldn't have gotten into a protracted conversation with Bill Buttering and left Sarah to do the sweeping all by herself. But he'd needed to get a few details settled about the paint and other supplies necessary to make the store acceptable, and there was still the matter of the floor that threatened to collapse. Furthermore, when Clint looked up at the ceiling, he could see pinpricks of sunlight that represented another set of problems.

The truth of the matter was, Clint was feeling sour on the whole idea of fixing up this shop and trying to do business in Big Pine. After all, damn near the whole town was gripped in mortal fear of Sheriff Mintner and his deputies. It was unlikely that they'd risk bringing Clint any gunsmithing business for fear of retaliation. But Clint recognized that he had a stubborn streak, and it forbade him from just riding out of town and letting Mintner and his bullies continue to dominate fine townspeople like Bill and Sarah.

Clint frowned at the poor job that Sarah had done on his uneven floor. Oh well. He set back to work with the broom, trying to remember to *move* the dirt instead making it become airborne.

He worked hard for the next few hours. After the sweeping, he used a bucket of water to scrub the walls in preparation for painting. Clint was handy with a saw, hammer, and nails, and it took him no time at all to right and repair the counter. It wasn't big enough, and he still needed to build a workbench, but that was a simple affair and his landlord had already promised him the available material.

By late afternoon, Clint decided that the little store had made quite a transition in its shabby appearance. It was clean, and he'd repaired the front door. Tomorrow, he'd get the panes of glass, have someone with that kind of experience set them in place, which would make a big difference. As for the floor, he'd scoot under the footings and see if he couldn't just shore up the sagging floor planks and leave it at that until he decided how long he was going to remain in business. Hell, he might not last a week in Big Pine given the daunting circumstances.

"Excuse me?"

Clint looked up to see Angie Buttering framed in the narrow doorway. The sun gilded her shapely outline and made her blond hair shine like spun gold. Clint set his hammer down and clucked his tongue in admiration. Angie might have been a coldhearted and scheming little gold digger, but she was also a real beauty. And despite Clint's misgivings about the young woman, he had to admit that he would love to make love to Miss Angie.

"Come on inside."

Angie stepped into the room. She daintily placed a foot down on what had been a sagging plank and tested it with her weight. "Still sags."

"Yep, but tomorrow I'll crawl underneath and prop the floor up in a few places. That'll be fine as a temporary repair. Your father and I both agree that, eventually, the entire floor needs to be replaced."

"You won't be in Big Pine long enough to worry about it," Angie said sweetly. "But I'll have to admit that you really have accomplished wonders in just one day."

"Thanks."

She offered him a quick and cold smile. "I remember I used to come in here and buy candy—this was a candy store while I was growing up. It was owned by an old couple named Henderson."

"What happened to them?"

"They got older and sicker. I think it was their diet. They both loved chocolate. That's about all they ate. Finally, Mrs. Henderson got real sick and died. After that, the old man ate up his inventory and then he closed shop and moved to Nebraska."

"I see."

Angie gazed around, but her blue eyes came to rest on the Gunsmith. "I guess you know that, by opening this store, you've put my father in the doghouse with Sheriff Mintner."

"I figure you can smooth that out," Clint said.

"As a matter of fact, I already have," Angie said, coming closer. "Why do you hate me, Mr. Adams?"

"I don't *hate* you, Miss Buttering. I just don't think you and I are going to be friends."

"You could be wrong."

"Not likely," he said, watching her eyes and seeing a frostiness creep into them. "You see, your father is a pretty straight shooter. I like that. He just wants to live in a town where people are happy and not warring with each other."

"I'm very happy in Big Pine."

"That's because you've sold out to Sheriff Mintner."

"Damn you!" she hissed. "I haven't sold out to anyone!"

"Oh? I saw you with the sheriff. Seems to me that you're a real pair of lovebirds. That bothers your father a whole lot more."

Her eyes glinted with anger. "Is that why my father has rented this . . . this hole-in-the-wall to you?"

"I guess it probably is," he admitted. "You see, parents are always the last to admit it when their children have gone bad."

"Why you arrogant—"

"Easy," Clint said, picking up his hammer and saw. "You don't want to say something that will just go to prove that you're no lady, do you?"

Angie Buttering visibly struggled to regain her composure. "You know," she managed to whisper, "I came in here hoping we might have a frank and constructive talk. I came in here convinced that I could talk you into leaving Big Pine before someone really got hurt."

"But you can't."

"No," she said, "I cannot. I've seen men like you before, Mr. Adams. They come—and they go. They never have anything of worth, and they all think they are fast with a gun and invincible. And sooner or later, they all leave town with their tails between their legs. They run to the next town seeking weakness to exploit."

"I'm not seeking weakness," Clint said, anger rising in his own voice. "I came here looking for a haven to recoup my good fortune. To make an honest dollar at a trade that I enjoy and am particularly good at. I came here looking to make a few new friends, and I have—but I've also found ruthless corruption and dishonorable people."

"Are you calling me ruthless?"

"If the shoe fits, wear it."

Angie's jaw muscles tightened. "I've already told my father what a stupid, even dangerous decision he made by renting this store to you, of all people."

"But he didn't listen to you any more than I did."

Angie smiled coldly. "Good-bye, Mr. Adams. I'd like to say that it's been pleasant talking to you and then wish you success in your new business. But the fact of the matter is that you won't be in business very long."

"That's for me to decide," Clint told the woman.

Angie turned on her heel and headed for the door. For some reason, she glanced up at the roof. Seeing the pinpricks of sunlight, she said, "I hope it rains as soon as you put out your equipment."

Clint laughed out loud at the young woman. "Come back anytime!" he called as she marched away.

He went to the door and admired the swing of her hips. Angie sure was a beauty. No wonder she was the one that Mintner had chosen to be his woman.

Clint went back into the little shop and picked up his hammer. He took a handful of nails and began to tighten the floor planks. After that, he would speak to Bill about material to patch the roof. With his luck, it probably would rain just about the time he opened for business.

At sundown, Clint went to the café to have dinner and visit Sarah, but she wasn't waitressing.

"What happened to Miss Taylor?" he asked the crabby old replacement who normally worked the morning shift.

"She isn't feeling well."

"Hmmm," Clint said. "That's news to me. She came by for a few minutes, and I had the feeling she was on her way to work. She looked to be feeling fine."

The woman looked askance at him. "Fine? She's got her neck out on the chopping block because of you, and you actually have the nerve to say that she looked to be feeling fine?"

Clint had started to sit down to eat but abruptly changed his mind. "Do you think she's been threatened because of me?"

The old woman's lips formed a hard, uncompromising line. "Mister, around here, it's healthiest not to say much of anything when it comes to the local politics. You understand?"

"Yeah," Clint said grimly before he headed for the door. "I understand."

He hurried up the street, and when he reached Sarah's shack, he banged on the door. "Sarah, are you in there?"

"Go away!"

Clint tried the door and discovered that it was barred from the inside. "Sarah! Open up!"

"Go away! Please!"

Clint reared back on one leg and kicked the door hard enough to bust inside. The interior of the room was dark, but there was a bedside candle burning, and it gave him enough light to see that Deputy Jed Cotton was lying bare-assed between Sarah's firm, white thighs.

"What the hell is wrong with you?" Jed yelled. "Can't you understand that *I'm* paying for this whore tonight?"

Clint swallowed and took a step back. He waited for Sarah to say something . . . anything. When she didn't, he turned on his heel and headed outside, feeling raw and angry.

"You're gonna pay to fix her door, too!" Jed yelled a moment before he began to laugh.

EIGHT

It stuck in Clint's craw all that evening that Sarah had taken Deputy Cotton to bed. It bothered him to think that she'd lied and, in fact, was probably just another lady for hire posing as a waitress. Clint did not entirely discount the fact that Sarah might have simply decided she had better move into the sheriff's camp in order to protect her own self-interest, but it still rankled. He felt betrayed.

That night he played a little poker, but he was in a foul mood and his luck was running bad. Clint lost three dollars and quit the game. He went over to the bar and ordered a double whiskey.

"Evening, Mr. Adams," the bartender said. "I heard that you're going to open a gunsmithing business."

"That's right."

"Might be a little slow in Big Pine. Might be that you could do a whole lot better somewhere else."

"You trying to talk me into leaving?"

The bartender was a small man in his forties, and Clint's rough tone startled him. "Oh, no sir! In fact, I got an old Navy six-shooter that I took to Sheriff Mintner for fixin'. He charged me five dollars, and the damn thing still don't shoot worth a tinker's damn!"

The bartender leaned closer. "But please don't tell the sheriff I said that!"

"I won't. Bring the Navy by my new shop tomorrow. I'll have a look at it and . . ."

"No, no! Listen," the bartender said under his breath so that no one else could hear, "I wouldn't be caught dead going into your shop. But if you come in tomorrow night, I'll slip that old six-shooter to you when no one is looking and—"

"To hell with that! If you haven't got the backbone to walk into my place of business like a free man, then I won't fix your damned old gun!"

The bartender blinked and looked quite offended. "Well, then, Mr. Adams, I believe there is no point in carrying on this conversation! I was only trying to—"

"I know what you were trying to do," Clint interrupted. "But I don't ask you to pour me a whiskey in the back room, do I?"

"No, but—"

"Then don't ask me to sneak around collecting guns that the sheriff couldn't fix."

Clint finished his whiskey in a foul mood and went outside. There was a warm wind blowing at the stars, and he felt restless, so he walked out to the edge of the town and then continued on another mile before he cooled down. He still had a few of Mintner's good cigars, and he lit one up and smoked it for the next hour, just lying on his back gazing up at the stars. He saw two shooters and took that to be a sign of good luck. Finally, relaxed and at peace, he climbed to his feet and walked back to town.

On an impulse, Clint angled past Sarah's shack. The door that he'd broken revealed a shaft of light, and curiosity made him edge up to it. "Sarah? You still got company?"

"Clint? Clint!"

Just the frightened tone of her voice told the Gunsmith that something was very wrong. He yanked the door open and stepped inside. Sarah was still lying on her bed, and her right eye was nearly swollen shut, her lips bruised and bloody.

"Goddamn!" Clint swore, sitting down at the bedside. "Did Cotton do this?"

Tears streaked her face. "He and the others."

"The others!"

"All the deputies but one had a turn," she choked, trying to hide her battered face.

Clint grabbed Sarah and turned her face up to him. "What happened? Why'd you go and ask Cotton in here in the first place?"

"He told me . . . never mind."

Clint shook the woman. "What the hell did he say? Come on, Sarah! What are you holding back?"

She looked up at him. "They said that they wanted to teach me a lesson in loyalty. They raped me and then said that if I messed around with you anymore——helped you in any way—they'd . . ."

Sarah couldn't finish and began to cry.

Clint cradled her head in his lap. "Sarah, Sarah," he whispered. "I'm sorry. This happened because you befriended me. And I didn't realize what a risk you were taking. I had no idea."

"Oh, let's just leave this awful town, Clint! Let's find a new place!" Sarah's voice took on hope. "We could stay together for a while, couldn't we? You could open your gunsmithing shop, and I can always find a job in some café. We're both good and we . . ."

But the Gunsmith gently placed a finger over her bruised lips. "Sarah," he said. "Is there a stage out of here?"

"Yes! And it leaves tomorrow!"

"Then you're going to be on it," he said. "I'll give you the ticket money, and when you get resettled, send me word where you are. I'll come for you and—"

"But you'll come too, won't you?"

"No," he told her. "After what they did to you, I'm going to stay here on principle. I won't leave until I've brought the whole damn rotten bunch of them to their knees."

She shook her head. "Oh, Clint! Don't say that! It isn't worth dying for! And we could . . ."

Once again, he silenced her. "Sarah, my mind is made up. You've got to go until this rough business is finished. Watching my own back is difficult enough without worrying about this sort of thing happening to you again."

She began to cry, but he remained firm. "Sarah, if I let this pass and ran away from Big Pine now, I'd never be able to look myself in the mirror again."

"Yes, you could!"

"No," he said gently but firmly, "I could not."

The Gunsmith went outside where there was a water pump and wet a cloth. He used it to clean Sarah's face. Her cuts and awful bruises made him more determined than ever to stay and fight Sheriff Mintner and his corruptness.

"Clint?"

"Yes?"

"There's a bottle of brandy that they didn't find hidden under this bed. Pour us a stiff drink, won't you?"

"Gladly. It's been a lousy day."

Clint knew where to find glasses, and he poured them each three fingers of brandy. Raising his glass in toast, he said, "To better days, Miss Taylor."

"To better days," she echoed in a thick voice.

They both tossed the brandy down, and Clint refilled their glasses. "So where are you going to go tomorrow?"

"Socorro," she told him. "It's the next good-sized town, and I've got a few friends there. I'll do fine. It's not me that I'm worried about."

"Don't worry about me," he told her. "I'm like a cat with nine lives."

"And how many have you used all those years you were a lawman?"

Clint grinned. "Maybe one or two."

"How many?"

"Three or four. I've still got an honest handful, Sarah."

She looked at him over her glass. "You ever get married?"

"Why don't we talk about us?" he suggested.

"All right," she said. "Where are you going to spend the night?"

"Back at my hotel room."

She took his hand. "Spend it with me. Please?"

"I don't think that would be such a good idea," he said.

"Clint, please don't leave me alone again in this town," she pleaded.

He studied her over the brandy. She looked rough and desperate.

"Bring me some water," she urged. "Let me clean up a little. Go for a short walk. I'll be ready for you in fifteen minutes."

"Sarah, I . . ."

"Please?"

"Oh, all right."

Clint brought her four buckets of water, and then he sauntered a short way over to the livery just to see how his black gelding was doing. A few minutes later, Clint strolled back to Sarah.

Only she was dead. Someone had plunged a knife into her chest. Her eyes were wide open, and although they were already beginning to glaze, Clint could see that they reflected stark terror.

"Oh, Jesus!" he moaned, dropping to one knee beside the bed and taking Sarah's lifeless hand. "Why on earth did I leave you even for a moment?"

Clint felt his eyes sting with grief. He hadn't known Sarah Taylor more than a couple of days, but she'd risked her life to befriend him and given of herself freely despite the danger.

"This changes things," Clint said, speaking softly to the dead woman. "Before, I was content just to bring Mintner and his deputies down. Now, I mean to destroy them! I'll find out which one of them did this to you, Sarah, and he'll die slow—that's a promise."

Clint reached for the bottle of brandy and poured himself another glass. There was no good sense in rushing out to find a deputy to shoot, they'd be there tomorrow, and besides, he'd need proof or he'd face a judge, jury, and hanging.

Proof. Now how in blazes was he going to get that? There were no witnesses. The sheriff and his deputies would just maintain that, with the busted door and all— a door that *he* had busted—someone must have come in to rob Sarah. She'd resisted, and the thief had murdered her. It was that simple.

Clint tossed down the brandy and poured another glass. Tears stung at his eyes. He wished to God that he had never heard of Big Pine. There were so many other towns in this fine New Mexico country that would have welcomed a good gunsmith with open arms. But he'd chosen this one, and even after things had started to sour, he'd gotten his back up and decided to stay and buck authority. And look what it had gotten poor dead Sarah.

But they would all pay.

NINE

Early the following morning, as Clint was dressing Sarah Taylor and preparing to go find the town's mortician, Sheriff Mintner and his three deputies arrived.

"Adams!" the sheriff called. "If you're in there, come on out!"

Clint stepped over to the shack's lone window and pulled the curtain aside. He saw Mintner flanked by his deputies and suddenly understood that he was about to be charged with the murder of Sarah Taylor. And given the injustice of the law here in Big Pine, it didn't take a lot of insight to figure out that he'd be tried by a corrupt judge and sentenced to hang.

With a jolt, Clint realized the seriousness of his predicament. And while he could not have left Sarah's body unattended, he could see that staying with her had placed his neck in a noose.

"Adams! We know that you're in there! Come on out!"

Clint studied the four men. He knew that Mintner was handy with a gun and a few of the others were probably halfway competent with a six-shooter, but he doubted that all four would stand up to a professional like himself.

Clint flexed his fingers and turned to look down at Sarah's poor, battered face. The bowie knife that had killed her lay on the counter, and she was wearing the best dress he had been able to find.

"Sarah, the first one I drop will be the sheriff," he promised. "Number two will be Jed Cotton. After that, I'll take as many as I can before they down me."

Unwilling to run, resigned to die if he had to, Clint touched Sarah's cold cheek and then stepped out of the shack. There was a small crowd behind the sheriff and his deputies. When they saw Clint appear, they moved out of the line of fire.

"Where is Miss Taylor?" the sheriff demanded.

"She was murdered last night by one of your deputies," Clint replied. "Sheriff, I'm counting on you to figure out which one of your men killed her."

Mintner rocked back on his heels. He glanced at the men who flanked him, then his eyes shifted back to the Gunsmith. "Seems to me that *you* are the prime suspect. Seems to me that *you* probably killed Miss Taylor."

"I thought you'd say that," Clint told the man. "But I didn't kill her."

"That's for a jury to decide."

"No," Clint said, a cold smile on his lips. "I guess it's for you to decide here and now."

Mintner blinked. "What the hell does that mean?"

"It means I'm not going to be arrested, and that one of your deputies murdered Miss Taylor."

"There are four of us and only one of you," Mintner said. "Hand over your gun."

Clint spread his feet a little wider apart. His hand moved closer to his gun butt. "Sheriff, either you make your play or you don't. Either way, the choice is yours, to live—or to die."

Mintner saw it now. He finally understood that the Gunsmith was willing to go down shooting and that he would not die alone. In fact, the sheriff realized with cold dread that he would be the first to fall in a bloody gunfight.

Cold sweat began to pour from Mintner's body. He could feel his heart slamming in his ears, and his toes and fingers started to tingle. He tried to swallow but couldn't. He wiped his sweaty palms on his pants and was acutely aware that his deputies were waiting for him to make the first move.

"Well, Sheriff?" the Gunsmith asked. "Are you going to die trying to arrest me—or decide that I'm above suspicion and that, as lawmen, we need to figure out which of your men murdered Sarah Taylor?"

"I didn't say that you killed her!" Mintner choked in a voice that he didn't recognize.

"Then I'm not under suspicion and you have no intention of arresting me? Is that it?"

The sheriff realized that he was having difficulty breathing and his legs felt weak. He wondered if he were having a heart seizure. My God! His father had died of heart trouble before he was forty years old.

"Sheriff!" Jed Cotton hissed. "Goddamn it! We can take him! There are *four* of us!"

"He's right," Clint said matter-of-factly. "There are four of you, and on my best day I wouldn't have been able to down you to the last man. I'd guess that two of you will live and two will die."

Clint sneered. "And imagine which group you'll be in, Sheriff. Cotton, my second bullet is inscribed with your name."

Jed Cotton paled, and the fight drained out of him. "She wanted me," he stammered. "Sarah liked me better'n you, Gunsmith. That ain't my fault!"

"You're a liar," Clint grated.

Deputy Cotton had been chewing on a toothpick, and now it spilled from his gaping mouth. "I swear I didn't stab her in the chest with that bowie knife!"

Clint raised his eyebrows. "Sheriff, did I say anything to you about a bowie knife in the chest?"

"No, but . . ."

"How did Deputy Cotton know that Miss Taylor was murdered with a bowie knife in the chest?"

Sheriff Mintner, cornered like a rat, suddenly saw an escape. Jumping back, he yelled, "Jed, you're under arrest for murder!"

"Oh no, you don't!" Cotton screamed, clawing for his six-gun.

Mintner beat him to it. The sheriff's hand streaked down to his holster and his six-gun came up level on Cotton before the deputy had cleared leather. The gun in Mintner's fist belched fire and smoke, and a bullet struck the deputy's chest, driving him backward. He tripped over his own heels, and when he struck the ground, they all heard the breath whoosh from his bullet-punctured lung.

Clint's own gun was already out and the hammer thumbed back, so that when the sheriff spun around with the intention of killing the Gunsmith, he found himself facing a drawn weapon.

"Don't shoot!"

"Of course not," Clint said, his six-gun steady on Mintner. "I was just backing your play. Now, why don't you make that clear to your deputies and tell them to go on back to the office?"

"You heard him," Mintner grated. The sheriff seemed to regain his composure. He looked around at the gathering crowd and shouted, "Everyone go about your business! I've got this under control!"

The crowd was slow to disperse. Women and children craned their necks to peer through the open door of Sarah Taylor's shack.

"Go on!" Mintner shouted. "I'll handle everything."

Clint led the sheriff inside the shack. Mintner studied the body, then turned to say, "Where is the murder weapon?"

"Over there on the counter."

Mintner found the knife. "Well, I'll be damned. This *was* Cotton's bowie."

Clint didn't believe that for a single moment. Jed Cotton had been reckless and a fool, but he had not been entirely stupid. Only an idiot would leave a very recognizable knife to reveal his identity. That led Clint to theorize that someone else had killed Sarah, then described the murder to the deputy in detail. But if that was not Jed Cotton's knife, then whose was it? The sheriff's?

"Yes," Mintner said, patting the flat of the knife's blade against his palm, "I've seen Jed use this before. He didn't carry it around much because of its size. But it was his, all right."

"Then that settles the issue," Clint said, pretending to believe him.

The sheriff looked at him closely. "Does it?"

"What do you mean?"

"I mean that I don't want any more trouble with you, Adams. In fact, if you'll give me your word to be peaceable, I'll even let you open that gunsmith shop."

"How generous."

"Don't smart-ass me, Adams!" Mintner snapped. "I *own* this town, and if you do business here, I'll own you, too."

"You got that dead wrong," Clint said. "And I'll open my business with—or without—your blessing."

Mintner didn't like hearing that one bit, but he managed to curb his anger. "Listen," he said, "we might be able to help each other."

"Why would we do that?"

"Why not? I could use one good deputy instead of three—make that two—useless ones. I pay each of them forty dollars a month. Tell you what, I'll fire 'em both and pay you what I paid them! How would you like to make eighty dollars a month?"

"That's a lot of money," Clint said, "but I don't think so."

"Why not?"

"I've got a gunsmithing shop to open today."

"Oh, hell! You won't make five dollars a day in a town this size, even if I do let everyone know that I approve."

Clint shrugged. "Whatever I make, it will be on my own hook, Sheriff."

Mintner sighed. "I don't understand. I've just offered you a chance to make lots more money than you'll make gunsmithing and you turn me down. Why?"

"I work for myself."

"You'd have the run of the town. I'd see that you were taken care of by the ladies. You'd have free drinks and get free food. You'd live better than you can imagine."

"Not interested."

"Damn it, why not?"

Clint was angry and reckless. "The truth?"

"Hell yes, the truth!"

"I don't like you."

The sheriff barked a laugh. "Finally, I believe you're speaking the truth."

"Don't matter to me if you believe it or not, Sheriff."

Mintner absently fingered the bowie that Clint had inspected so carefully. It was a cheap, nondescript weapon, not even very sharp. It had a cracked wooden handle. Every year there were thousands of these poor quality knives mass-produced in the East and sold for less than five dollars. One could find them in every trading post and general store between the muddy Mississippi and the Pacific Ocean.

The sheriff's eyes kept shifting from Clint to the knife and back again. The Gunsmith was sure that the man was measuring his chances of putting the cheap bowie in Clint's chest and then probably claiming he'd acted in self-defense.

Finally, however, Mintner said, "What has liking or disliking each other to do with the business of making money? I want your gun, not your damned friendship."

"My gun is not for sale."

"It always has been!" Mintner lowered his voice. "Listen, you still haven't got a pot to piss in after all the years you've given of loyal service to one damn thankless sheriffing job after another. I'm offering you a chance to make some *real* money."

"I'll think on your offer," Clint said, knowing he had to play this man like a fish in order to learn who really murdered Sarah Taylor.

"Well," Mintner blustered, stung by Clint's lack of enthusiasm. "I ain't goin' to keep that offer open forever, I'll tell you for damned sure!"

"Just don't try and warn people off from getting me to fix their guns."

Mintner wheeled about and marched over to the bed where Sarah was lying. "She looks pretty beat-up."

"Your deputies did that," Clint said, struggling to keep his voice under control. "They beat her up and raped her."

"You can't rape a whore," the sheriff stated. "You can cheat a whore out of her money, but you can't rape her."

"She wasn't a whore," Clint said through clenched teeth, "and she was raped."

Mintner turned. "If you're thinking about killing my men, then I tell you this—you'll hang. Rapin' and beatin' up a loose woman isn't considered to be all that damned important in Big Pine."

"Get the hell out of here," Clint hissed, "before I go ahead and shoot you after all."

The sheriff started to bluster, but when he saw the look on the Gunsmith's face, he changed his mind. "I don't think I'd want you as a deputy anyway," he said as he left the room.

Clint realized that his hands were shaking with rage. He found the brandy and dispensed with a glass by drinking it straight from the bottle. The brandy steadied his nerves, but it didn't quench his thirst for revenge.

"Give 'em time," he said to himself. "Give 'em just enough rope to hang themselves."

Clint took another long pull on the bottle and then headed off to find the mortician. He would, of course, use the very last of his poker winnings to give Sarah a proper burial. Maybe she had even stashed away a few dollars of her own to help defray expenses, but he doubted it.

When Clint found the mortician, who also served as the town's only dentist, the man was still in bed, asleep. Clint had to bang on his door, squabble with his upset wife, and then threaten to come inside and drag the mortician out of bed before he could get the man's attention.

After a quick introduction with very few facts, Clint asked, "How much will a decent funeral cost?"

"Fifty dollars."

"Do it for ten," Clint said. "And I want a good casket, not some damned pine box."

"It can't be done for ten lousy dollars!"

Clint knew better. Lawmen learned the cost of burials, and ten dollars would buy a good one.

"Let's put it this way," Clint said. "This woman had very little money, and I'm not exactly flush myself. That being the case, you are going to underwrite this funeral at your own expense."

"Why should I?"

Clint drew his six-gun and used it to prod the mortician in the belly. "Because," he said, "if you don't, I might be forced to underwrite *your* funeral."

The mortician's eyes fluttered, and his face turned milk-white. "Yes, sir!"

"Good," Clint said, holstering his gun. "I'll tell everyone that knew Sarah that the funeral will take place this afternoon."

"But . . ."

Clint dug the last of his money from his pockets and slapped it down against the mortician's granite slab. "I'll see you later," he said, leaving the man. "I've got a gunsmithing business to open and a lot to do in preparation. If you need good work at a reasonable price, I'm your man."

"I don't even own a gun! I don't believe in firearms."

"Figures," Clint said. Outside, he took a deep breath of fresh air and went to his shop.

Bill Buttering hurried over. "I heard about Miss Taylor and that you were more than a little involved."

"That's right. They murdered Sarah, and they planned to make me the scapegoat. It would have been neat, except that I managed to ruin their plans."

"How?"

"I let them know that I would rather go down with a gun smoking in my fist than a noose around my neck."

"Oh," Buttering said, "I see."

Clint wanted to get his mind off Sarah and her tragic death. He needed a little time to clear his thoughts and make his plans on how he would find the real killer and then what he was going to do in retaliation.

"If you'll excuse me," he said, removing his jacket and rolling up his sleeves, "I've got a floor to brace."

"Need some help?"

"No thanks," Clint said, grabbing some blocks that he'd sawed the day before and then shimmying under the floor where he intended to wedge the blocks between the hard-packed earth and his shop's rotting floorboards.

TEN

When the Gunsmith figured that he had his flooring braced as well as could be expected, he crawled out from under the little shop, dusted off his clothes, and watched as a lank, tobacco-chewing man in his thirties began to replace his front window.

"I also paint signs," the man said, without turning from his delicate work. "For three dollars, I'll draw you a sign on this here window sayin' that you are a gunsmith. But you'll have to spell it fer me."

"Sorry, but I'm a little short of cash right now," Clint said. "Besides, I guess that everyone in town knows that I'm opening a gunsmithing business in Big Pine."

"Might be the truth," the man said, setting the pane of glass into the framework, then using putty to mold it into place. "Besides, I got a hunch that you won't be around very long."

Clint bristled. "I keep hearing that, and I'm getting a little annoyed. The fact of the matter is that Sheriff Mintner and I have made peace."

"That right?" The man did not turn or sound particularly interested as he spat a stream of tobacco on the wall.

"That's right. In fact, he's given me his blessing."

"I doubt it," the man said. He turned to look at Clint. He was gangly with a hangdog expression and dull eyes. He gave the impression of being neither intelligent nor ambitious. "Did you really face him and the other deputies down this morning with that there hogleg?"

"I don't know if I'd put it that way," Clint said. "I think what we had was a meeting of the minds. A decision that we'd all rather live than die."

"Huh!" The man scratched his day-old beard and squinted with puzzlement. "Huh!"

"Do you have any guns that need to be worked on?"

"Have an old Kentucky rifle."

"Well, I . . ."

"But the barrel is broke and the hammer fell off a couple of years ago. Thing never did shoot straight noway."

"Anything else?"

The man thought long and hard. "Got an old Army Colt."

"I've worked on hundreds of them. Fine weapons."

"Not mine, fer sure. The dern thing blew all to hell last time it was fired. All six chambers exploded together."

"You're extremely lucky not to have lost your gun hand."

"Wasn't me that fired it. Was my brother, Elwin. Maybe you seen him hereabouts? One-handed fella with black powder burns pittin' his face and his lower lip sorta blowed off."

"No," Clint said, wishing he'd never engaged this idiot in conversation, "I haven't yet had the pleasure."

"He's sort of strange. Don't like folks much. Don't have no gun, either."

Clint went inside the shop before the man gave him a monumental headache. With white paint and a brush, the Gunsmith attacked the walls with vigor. He wanted to finish them in time to clean up and get to Sarah's funeral, which was scheduled for one o'clock.

Clint didn't like painting and was sloppy because he was in such a hurry. But the room was small, and by working at top speed, he finished the distasteful work by noon and then went next door to the general store to get some kerosene to clean himself.

"Well," Buttering said, studying Clint's paint-streaked face with amusement, "did you also manage to get some paint on the walls?"

"I did," Clint said. "You coming to the funeral?"

"I can't leave the store. I'm sure sorry to hear about Miss Taylor, though. She was tough, but always nice. I liked and respected her."

"She was a good woman," Clint said, beginning to scrub the paint off of himself. "By the way, do you know if Deputy Cotton carried a bowie knife?"

"Is that what killed Miss Taylor?"

"Yes."

"Well," Buttering said, "I don't believe that Jed did wear a bowie knife."

"What about the other deputies?"

The store owner's brow knitted in silent concentration. "Let's see, now. There's Bob Bogard, but he don't wear a knife. Jed Cotton is dead as of this mornin', and that leaves . . . yeah, that new fella with the handlebar mustache. His name is Jim Wild. Now, I believe he does wear a bowie knife."

"Are you sure?"

"No, I'm not," Buttering admitted. "The man hasn't been in town more than a couple of months. I get the feeling he had quite a reputation as a gunman down in Texas. He dresses fancy and wears his gun tied down. He has silver spurs and wears 'em all the time, though

I've never seen him horseback. Them fancy spurs have
little jinglebobs on the rowels, and he likes to make them
sing as he struts down the boardwalk lookin' like he owns
the whole damn world. People give him plenty of room,
I tell you."

"I remember him. He was going to be the third man I
tried to drop if the shooting began this morning outside
of Sarah's place."

"He's supposed to be real fast," Buttering said. "I mean,
probably not near as fast as you, but fast all the same."

"He has the look of a shooter," Clint agreed. "I doubt
that he'll be pushed."

"I doubt it, too," Buttering said. "He strikes me as a
real prideful man."

Clint agreed. He also reluctantly concluded that a dandy
like Jim Wild would not wear a cheap bowie knife. He was
the kind that would have a very fancy one, probably with
a polished elk's horn handle or some such showy thing.

"When you see Jim Wild," Buttering said, as Clint
finished removing the paint from his hands, arms, and
face, "you'll probably discover that he wears a knife.
But I'm not sure. Maybe you should ask someone else.
Ask Dominic. He's the fellow that's putting in your new
window."

"I doubt Dominic could help me," Clint said. "The man
doesn't seem especially observant."

"Well, that's true," Buttering said with a knowing grin.
"Dominic and his brother just sort of . . . exist. They do
odd jobs, although most people steer clear of Dominic's
brother, Elwin."

"He's the one that had his hand blown off when his
six-gun exploded?"

"You heard about that, huh?"

"I did," Clint said.

"Well, Elwin is sort of a sneaky son of a bitch, and he's got a real vicious side. Whenever he gets a few spare dollars in his pocket, he gets drunk and raises hell. He's a big bastard, and he gets an ax handle and sets out to destroy everything in his path. Before that happens, Sheriff Mintner and his boys generally gang-tackle him and throw him in jail until he sobers up. He's only one-handed—like me—but he's mean and damned strong. Drunk or sober, Big Elwin doesn't know the meaning of fear. When he and Dominic get into a fight, you'd better clear out."

"Those two sound like quite a pair."

"Oh, Dominic is all right. He's a steady but slow worker who keeps pretty much to himself. He and his brother own a shack about a mile south of town, but nobody in their right mind would ever pay 'em a social visit."

"Well," Clint said, "I'd best get back to the hotel and change into my best clothes for Sarah's funeral."

"You sorta took a shine to her, didn't you?"

"You could say that."

"To be honest, I sorta liked her myself. Once, I even considered . . . well, never mind."

"Yeah," Clint said, as he turned to leave.

Forty-five minutes later the Gunsmith was standing in the cemetery with Dan Hurley, the cranky waitress, Sheriff Mintner, and a handful of other friends waiting for the hearse to arrive and the funeral services to get under way.

Young Dan Hurley said, "My grandpa and the mortician are loading the casket onto a buckboard. Grandpa will be driving it out here."

"She was good woman," a shabby, heavyset man intoned. "Sarah had a kind and a generous heart. She'd loan you a dollar whenever you were hungry—or thirsty."

"That's right," a gray-faced, frail-looking man who reeked of whiskey said. "Whenever I had the shakes, Sarah would give me free coffee and a seltzer. She was like a saint, I tell you!" Tears rolled down the man's dirty cheeks. "I just wish that we knowed fer sure who killed her! I'd kill *him*!"

"Sure you would," the sheriff snapped. "Pete, you're so damned drunk and messed up you can't kill your own body lice."

Pete's bloodshot eyes radiated hatred. "Sheriff, you're the one that's supposed to . . . to do something!"

Mintner's hands balled at his sides and he leaned in close to the drunkard. "Pete! Have you completely lost your mind? Jed Cotton stabbed Sarah to death with his bowie knife. I already shot him. Remember?"

Pete's rage dissolved into confusion, then surprise. "You did?"

"That's right. Sarah's murderer was my deputy. I take the blame for that, and I settled the score."

"Oh." Pete dredged up a toothless smile. "Well, in that case, I think we ought to have a drink and celebrate!"

"Pete, get away from me before I have one of my deputies run you the hell out of Big Pine."

"But I always lived here! I lived here since I was a kid."

"Maybe you need to expand your horizons."

"Aw, I don't think so, Sheriff. Please don't send me away! I don't know nobody nowhere else."

Clint watched the man begin to snivel. "Sheriff, why don't you let him be? Pete is here for the same reason we all are—to pay his last respects to Sarah Taylor."

The sheriff pinned Clint with a cold glare. "Maybe you better tend to the business of mourning and let me . . ."

"Here comes Grandpa!" Dan shouted. "Here comes Mr. Divel, too!"

The sheriff turned away from the Gunsmith, cheeks red with anger. Clint forgot about Mintner and waited as the buckboard approached. When he saw that it contained two caskets, he was furious and knew at once that the mortician had decided to cut his costs of transportation by bringing Jed Cotton's body along with that of Sarah Taylor. Both were resting in cheap pine boxes.

When the buckboard pulled into the cemetery, the mortician said, "We'll have a combined service for Miss Taylor and Mr. Cotton. Afterward, we'll all join together in hymn and—"

"Like hell we will!" Clint thundered. "This is Sarah's funeral, bought and paid for!"

"For ten dollars, you're lucky I didn't bury them in the same grave," Divel retorted in a snippy tone.

Clint reached up and grabbed the man by the front of his black suit and jerked him completely off the seat of the buckboard. He spilled the mortician to the earth and then drew back his fist and hissed, "You're not a very smart man, are you? Now I want—"

"Freeze!"

Clint turned to see Sheriff Mintner's gun barrel pointed at his head.

"On your feet," the sheriff ordered.

Clint released the squirming mortician and stood. He turned to face Mintner and knew that, if they had been alone, the sheriff would have shot him without a moment's hesitation.

"Sheriff, I paid ten dollars for a decent funeral for Sarah. This man puts her in a three-dollar pine box and tries to make it a joint funeral."

"He paid me a lousy ten dollars, Sheriff!" Divel squealed, jumping to his feet and slapping the dust from his jacket. "Ten dollars, and he expects me to bury her as if she was the Queen of England instead of just a two-bit whore that—"

The back of Clint's hand swept out and caught Divel flat-footed. Clint hit him in the mouth with such force that the man was lifted off his feet and crashed into the buggy, striking his head against its side. The mortician crumpled to the ground, and Clint did not blink or remove his eyes from the sheriff's face.

"I could arrest you for assault," the sheriff said. "I could put you in jail and throw away the key."

"You could, but it would be a very bad idea," Clint told the sheriff.

"Give me one good reason why."

Clint thought fast. "Because I have lawmen friends all over New Mexico and Texas that would come and set me free. And if you tried to stop them, they'd kill you with as little concern as if they were stepping on a bug."

"Is that right?"

"That's right," Clint said, doubting if it were true, but playing the bluff, knowing that his life depended upon it. "Sheriffs and marshals watch out for each other, Mintner. But that's something you wouldn't know because you're a disgrace to the profession."

The gun in Mintner's fist trembled. Then Mintner said under his breath, "You're becoming a real thorn in my side. You better hope your business fails and you ride out of town before you have a fatal accident."

Clint turned his back on the man and said to the others, "Help me get Sarah's casket out of that buckboard. There are shovels aplenty. Let's get this over with and return to our businesses."

Pete and the heavyset man looked to Sheriff Mintner, and when he nodded his approval, they jumped forward to help the Gunsmith. In less than fifteen minutes, the grave was dug and fitted with the pine box.

"Ahem," the mortician said, coming to stand beside the grave with his Bible in his bony hands. "Dear Lord, I—"

"Shut up," Clint growled. "You want to preach, do it over Jed Cotton after we're gone and you've dug his damned grave."

Clint removed his black Stetson and bowed his head. "Dear Lord," he began, "I hardly knew this woman, but it was easy to tell she had a good and generous heart. Now someone stabbed her to death, and while it might have been Jed Cotton, I'm not convinced of the fact. But I'll find out who *did* kill Miss Taylor, and then I hope you'll have mercy on his soul 'cause I'm sending his body to hell."

Clint took a deep breath. He glanced over at the sheriff, who was staring at him. Clint cleared his throat. "Lord, Big Pine is a corrupt town. You know that, and so does everyone else. But we're going to do some housecleaning. We're going to cast out the evil and save the righteous. Give me the wisdom to know which is which before I kill 'em all. Amen."

Clint returned his hat to his head, and when he saw Mintner's face, he knew that he had cut the sheriff to the core and that one of them was going to be buried in this lonesome cemetery before a week passed.

"That's it?" the fat man asked, sweating profusely. "That's all you got to say?"

"That's all," Clint replied. "But there's nothing the Lord would like better than for each of you to add your own words before you lay poor Sarah to rest."

The fat man looked to Pete, who gulped and said, "Let's just cover her up, Joe. Sarah was a good old girl, but all the words in the world won't help her now."

The fat, shabby man nodded and began to shovel. Clint glanced at Mintner, then started walking back to town.

"Wow!" young Dan Hurley cried, overtaking him. "I can't believe what happened back there! I thought you were a cooked goose when the sheriff got the drop on you."

"So did I," Clint confessed. "I made a bad mistake, losing my temper and letting him get his gun out like that. A mistake that would have cost me my life if you and everyone else hadn't been standing there as witnesses to what would have been an outright murder."

"But your lawmen friends would have come and evened the score, huh?"

"That's right," Clint said. "They'd have made certain that justice was served."

"Wow! No offense, Mr. Gunsmith, but I sure would have liked to have seen that! I mean, you probably count Wyatt Earp, Ben Thompson, Wild Bill Hickok, and the whole bunch of 'em as your best friends, huh?"

"For a fact," Clint said, not wanting to disappoint the young man.

"Jeez," the kid breathed. "I sure would like to meet those fellas! You expect that, if you have to take on Sheriff Mintner and his deputies, you'll call 'em in to help?"

Clint thought a moment and then said, "What makes you think I haven't already called in one or two?"

Dan's eyes grew round with excitement. "Jeez!" he whispered. "Wyatt Earp, Ben Thompson, Wild Bill Hickok! Which ones?"

"You'll know if and when they arrive," Clint said, suppressing a smile as they returned to town. He would give anything to see Mintner and his deputies' faces when they heard this rumor.

"See ya later!" Dan said, practically jumping up and down before he dashed off to spread the word about the impending arrival of Clint's famous lawmen friends.

The sight of the boy racing up the street caused the Gunsmith to smile despite his grim and worrisome circumstances. Only now did he realize that part of the reason he'd stubbornly refused to ride on was that he'd wanted to show Sarah Taylor that he could still clean up a town in spite of long odds. To make her see that the law, when it turned against the people, was wrong and it would be overthrown.

But Sarah was dead, and he had told everyone that he was opening a business. A business that really had no chance of success, but he'd still open it and put on a brave front. Now, he was going to save Big Pine for himself, for Bill Buttering, and for the rest of the community's good people who were being bullied, extorted, and—in poor Sarah Taylor's case—even murdered.

ELEVEN

Clint wasn't able to get his gunsmith shop open that day, and perhaps it was just as well; his spirits were very low. He did manage to get the door fixed and a workbench built and decided that he would open for business the following morning. It would be on a Wednesday, and that would give him four days to test Big Pine's business climate. Maybe he'd give his little enterprise the rest of this week and all of next. If, by then, he still hadn't won over the townspeople's trust, then he'd pack up and leave for Santa Fe where he was sure that the business climate would be a whole lot healthier.

But Clint knew that packing up and leaving would have to wait until he had settled the score with Sheriff Mintner and the deputies who had beaten and raped poor Sarah. And there was still the matter of figuring out who had murdered the poor woman. Clint had already made note of the fact that, while Jim Wild did pack a bowie knife, it was too fancy to be the murder weapon. Besides, Wild did not seem like the kind of a man who would either rape or stab a woman to death. And while Clint could not exactly say why he had formed that opinion of the dandy, it was strongly held. That left Bob Bogard.

That evening when Clint was spending the last of his money on a modest dinner, he saw an opportunity to talk to Deputy Wild when the man came in to eat by himself.

"Mind if I join you?" Clint asked, bringing his coffee cup over to Jim Wild's table.

"Yeah, I mind."

"Thanks," Clint said, taking a seat as if he had not been rebuffed.

Wild flushed with anger but kept himself under control and said, "You aren't exactly welcome in Big Pine. But I suppose that much ought to be obvious even to someone like yourself."

"Sarah Taylor wasn't afraid to make up her own mind about who she wanted as a friend."

"Maybe she thought you had money. Maybe she lost her senses." Wild, a handsome young man with perfect teeth and a drooping handlebar mustache, frowned. "How would I know what she saw in you? What I *do* know is that it probably got her killed."

"Keep talking," Clint ordered.

Wild leaned back in his chair and folded his arms over his chest. "I ain't saying another word."

"Sarah said that all the deputies but one raped her. Are you that one?"

Wild drew in a deep breath and expelled it slowly. "Mister," he said, "I will tell you this just one time. I ain't never paid a woman for it, and I never took it by force. Women have always come to *me*, not the other way around. With Sarah, it weren't no different."

Clint looked deep into the man's unflinching gray eyes. "All right," he said. "Then besides Jed Cotton, it was Bogard who used Sarah?"

"I didn't say that!"

"You didn't have to," Clint snapped. "He raped her and he'll pay. Now, what I want to know is, did he also murder her?"

Jim Wild leapt out of his chair. "I've lost my appetite. I'm getting the hell out of here."

"Not," Clint said, hand coming to rest on his gun butt, "unless you're prepared to get past me."

Wild looked toward the door, searching in vain for help. Seeing no one, he slowly raised his hands up around his chest and looked toward the kitchen where the owner was standing with his jaw hanging open.

"Mr. Tabor, if he guns me down, you remember what you saw."

Clint relaxed. He even smiled. "I'm not going to gun you down, Deputy. All I want is some answers."

"Well, I haven't got any! All I can tell you is that I didn't put that knife in Sarah Taylor's chest, and I doubt that the others did either!"

"Then maybe the sheriff himself killed her."

"You can believe whatever you want," Wild said, "but I'll tell you one thing, I don't rape, and I don't kill women. I don't even beat 'em up. I swear that's the truth."

"So, if it wasn't any of you fellows, who did kill Sarah?"

"I don't know, and I don't much care," the deputy sneered. "She wasn't that much of a woman anymore. Probably still pretty good in bed but—"

Clint's right hand shot up and crashed against the deputy's jaw, and the man backpedaled into the street. He bounced off a hitching post, steadied himself, and then spat blood.

"You man enough to fight me with fists?"

"Damn right," Clint said, stepping out of the café and moving swiftly across the boardwalk with his fists raised.

Wild spat more blood and came in swinging. He was strong, fast, and his punches were measured and crisp. The Gunsmith took two straight jabs to the face, ducked an overhand right, and pounded the deputy in the solar plexus. Wild's cheeks puffed outward and his mouth flew open. He grunted in pain, and the Gunsmith closed in with a smashing left that sent the deputy sprawling in the street.

Wild wasn't finished. Pushing himself up on all fours, he lunged at the Gunsmith and managed to get his arms around Clint's knees and tackle him to the dirt.

"I'll break you!" Wild screamed, pounding at Clint's face like a man gone crazy.

The Gunsmith blocked most of the wicked punches, and when Wild began to gasp for breath, Clint retaliated. They rolled, punching and gouging furiously. Clint was fortunate to end up on top when they slammed into a hitching post. Rearing up on his knees, he pounded Deputy Wild three times in the face, breaking nose, teeth, and lips. The man howled and bucked, but Clint grabbed him by the throat and squeezed until his eyes bulged.

"Quit!" Clint shouted.

But when the deputy slammed a fist into the Gunsmith's kidney, Clint delivered the knockout punch. Wild, his face covered with blood, quivered and choked. Clint climbed off the man and dragged him over to a horse trough. Pulling Wild over the lip of the water trough, he dunked the man's head into the mossy horse trough and held it under until Wild began to thrash.

Clint yanked the man back and let him drop. "If I see you again, you'd better go for your gun," Clint grated. "That's fair warning that you need to get out of town."

Climbing unsteadily to his feet, the Gunsmith walked toward his hotel. People cleared a wide path for him, and when he entered the lobby, all conversation stopped and the hotel's boarders gaped.

"Bring me up a bath as well as a cold basin of water and plenty of towels," Clint mumbled as he headed for his room. "And Epsom salts!"

"Yes, sir!"

That night the Gunsmith not only locked his hotel room door but also dragged the bed in front of it so that he would not have the sheriff and his one remaining healthy deputy bursting into his room. And despite a good soaking, he awoke late the next morning feeling as if he had been beaten by clubs. His knuckles were stiff, skinned, and swollen. He could not have drawn his gun in a hurry to save his life.

He limped over to his door, threw it open, and yelled, "Bring me another bath and more salts!"

The bath and buckets of steaming water arrived in less than fifteen minutes. Clint added the soaking salts and spent the next hour trying to decide if he should even bother to attempt to open his shop this morning or if he should show good sense and just leave Big Pine while he was still capable of going under his own power.

By the time his bathwater was cold, the Gunsmith had decided that he had to remain in Big Pine until Sarah's murderer was caught and he had repaid Bogard for his ruthless treatment of Sarah. To do anything less would be inexcusable.

He was just finishing dressing when a pounding on his door brought the Gunsmith around and reaching for his Colt. "Who is it?"

"Sheriff Mintner! Open up!"

"What do you want?"

"We're going to talk!"

"Talk?"

Clint breathed in deeply and massaged his bruised knuckles. As much as it galled to admit the fact, he was a few years past his prime when it came to fistfighting. This morning he dearly wished he had simply pistol-whipped the younger Deputy Wild and then he wouldn't be suffering.

"Yeah, talk!"

Clint checked his pistol, and then he grabbed his bed and pulled it aside. When he gripped the doorknob, he made sure he was not in the line of fire just in case Mintner and his deputy had it in mind to shoot him on sight.

Cocking back the hammer of his six-gun, Clint pushed the door open and remained out of the line of possible fire.

"Don't worry," Mintner growled, "I'm not loaded for bear. I came to talk."

Clint eased around the corner of the door to see Mintner and Bogard. Clint said, "Send your boy packing, Sheriff."

Mintner looked at his deputy and nodded. When Bogard started to protest, Mintner said, "I'll be all right. Go along now!"

"Come inside," Clint said, using the barrel of his Colt to motion the sheriff into his small room before he closed the door. "Have a seat on the bed."

Mintner did as he was ordered. His eyes went to the bath and then to Clint's face, which was puffy on the right side and definitely bruised. "You look like you've been in a fight, but compared to Jim Wild, you haven't anything to complain about."

"How is he?"

"He's gone," Mintner said. "His face is damn near unrecognizable. I sent him up to Santa Fe where there's a doctor who will try and put his nose back in place. I'll tell you one thing, he'll have to pay for his *next* woman."

"That bad, huh?"

"Yeah," the sheriff said. "But don't feel sorry for him. He beat the hell out of a few men and treated women like farm animals."

Clint sighed. "I should have pistol-whipped the man and been done with it instead of each of us trying to beat the other's brains out on the dirt."

"Wild was a vicious fighter," Mintner said. "I was surprised that you were able to whip him. He looks— I mean looked—like a dandy, but he was tougher than rawhide."

"I won't be arrested. It was a fair fight," Clint said.

"I didn't come to arrest you. I came to offer you that deputy's job one more time. I'm getting kinda short on 'em."

Clint stared at the man, not sure if his leg was being pulled.

"The job is still open, and the money is still good," Mintner said.

"All I want to do is find out who murdered Sarah."

"It wasn't me or any of my deputies, I promise you that."

Clint holstered his six-gun. "All right, let's say I believe you. Who else would have killed her?"

The sheriff shrugged his shoulders. "I don't know."

"Well . . ."

"But," the sheriff interrupted, "if you come to work for me, you'd have free rein to investigate and find out. And I expect, if you're half the lawman you're made out to be, you'll find the killer."

"I don't get it," Clint said. "Why hire me?"

"I told you, I need deputies. And I'd rather have some-one as tough as you working *for* me."

Mintner rose to his feet and rubbed his jaw. There were dark circles around his bloodshot eyes, and when he raised his hand to run his fingers through his hair, Clint saw that they trembled. It told him that Mintner had had a long night and had been drinking heavily.

"Fish or cut bait," Mintner said, heading for the door.

"And that means?"

"Either take my job offer or when I return it will be with Deputy Bogard, and we'll be gunning for you."

"That could be fatal."

"Yeah," Mintner said, "we'll both probably be dead before the gun smoke clears. But you've put my back against a wall, and I'm not backing up any farther."

Clint watched the sheriff leave his room.

TWELVE

Three days later, Clint got tired of sitting on the front porch of his gunsmith shop and watching dogs fornicate, kids play, women shop, and people watch him doing nothing but slipping deeper into debt. The Hurleys had brought him a few old weapons that needed minor fixing, and he'd traded that work against Duke's mounting feed bill. Bill Buttering had also tried to give him a little work and a lot of credit. But beyond that, Clint hadn't seen a dime's worth of business from the rest of the citizenry.

At least five or six times a day, Deputy Bogard would pass by with a sneer on his lips that got Clint's blood boiling. It was all the Gunsmith could do not to brace and then either shoot or humiliate the man.

Almost as vexing was to see Sheriff Mintner with Miss Angie Buttering on his arm. She never failed to avoid Clint's gaze, but once or twice, when she thought he was not watching, he'd caught her looking in his direction.

"It breaks my heart to see them together," Bill Buttering lamented. "Mintner is too old, too rich, and too corrupt for my daughter."

"Maybe he's too old and too corrupt," Clint said, "but I can't see how anyone could ever be too rich."

"It's not the fact that he has a lot of money," Buttering said with bitterness, "it's the way that he comes by it that gets my goat. Like I told you, Mintner has broken a lot of people just to pick their pockets before he drove them out of Big Pine. He's a ruthless businessman who has gone mad with power."

"Why didn't he get your general store? It's probably the most profitable business in town, perhaps with the exception of the bigger saloons."

"He would have swallowed me up like the others if he hadn't been sweet on Angie."

"So," Clint said, "you're caught in a dilemma."

"I'd trade everything I own and leave Big Pine without a penny in my pocket if I could save my daughter from that man's clutches," Buttering proclaimed. "She's all that I care about now, and she's being swallowed up by his greed and power."

Buttering looked at Clint. "You're about my last hope, Clint. If you decide to ride out of town, I think my Angie is lost."

The Gunsmith shook his head. "I don't think that's necessarily true," he told the man. "Angie will eventually see what kind of man the sheriff really is."

"Sure, after she has two or three of his kids. Then what? Kids have to have a father. Mothers can't live on their own in these hard times. What would Angie do?"

"Listen," Clint said, seeing how upset the storekeeper was becoming, "I think that you're getting worked up over something that might not even happen."

"It will, unless you step up and steal her away from Mintner."

Clint could see that it was useless to carry on this depressing conversation, so he tried to change the subject.

"I can't sit around here much longer, Bill. I have to do something."

"Why, you've only been open for a few days! What's the hurry?"

"Nothing will happen unless I make some changes," Clint said stubbornly. "And what I'm about to say isn't going to please you."

"Then don't say it."

"I have to," Clint said. He scowled, seeking the words to put his feelings across to this man who had become his friend. "Bill, I want to show Mintner up and make a go of it in Big Pine, but, even more, I want to find out who murdered Sarah."

"How?"

Clint shrugged. "As a gunsmith, when I ask questions, people just clam up and give me a go-to-hell look. But if I was a deputy then . . ."

"What?"

"Settle down," Clint said, placing a hand on Buttering's thin shoulders. "Hear me out, Bill. The sheriff has asked me to be his deputy."

"You'd sell your soul to the devil?"

"No," Clint said, "but he has offered me eighty dollars a month."

"But he's crooked!"

"Hold your voice down," Clint said, seeing people up and down the main street turn and stare. "Sure, Mintner is crooked. But as a deputy, I can pin on a badge and have the authority to conduct an investigation into Sarah Taylor's murder. It would also allow me the pleasure of watching the sheriff fire Bob Bogard. And if he protested, then I'd have the chance to give him a little payback for what he did to Sarah."

Buttering's face pinched with despair. "Yes, but . . ."

"And another thing," Clint said. "If I were deputy, I could snoop around a little and find out exactly what kind of mischief the sheriff is up to and perhaps get some hard evidence against him. It might be the answer to your prayers, Bill."

The storekeeper had been about to speak, but now he pursed his lips thoughtfully. "Yes," he said. "But tell me this, why would Mintner hire you?"

"I've asked myself the same question. Maybe he wants to keep a close eye on *me*. I don't know for sure."

"Hard to say," Buttering said.

Clint nodded. "Sometimes a smart man hires his worst enemy and turns him into his best ally. I think that Mintner believes that he can buy me for a high salary and maybe even a little extortion money. Money corrupts, Bill."

"But not you."

Clint chuckled. "I haven't sold out, but they say every man does have his price."

"Bullshit!"

"Well," Clint said with a broad grin, "whether you believe it or not, the sheriff is a smart man, and I think he'd much rather see me with him than against him."

"I just don't know," Buttering said quietly.

"It's either that," Clint said, "or I'm going to have to pack my bags and ride. I won't live on charity, and I'm sure not going to live on gunsmithing in Big Pine."

"I don't mind carrying you, no matter how long it takes."

"No," Clint said. "I wouldn't feel right about it, even if I did think that things would eventually change. But they wouldn't. Al Mintner didn't get a stranglehold on this town in a few months, and I won't break it that soon either—not unless I can prove that he's been swindling, extorting, and cheating people. And to do that I'm going to have to work out of his office."

"That's the only way?"

Clint nodded. "The only way."

Bill Buttering's mouth turned down at the corners. "Maybe," he said, arguing to himself, "if you were a deputy, you'd see more of Angie and could eventually . . ."

"Not a chance!" Clint said. "You've got a fine daughter, but if I paid the least bit of attention to Angie, I'd get fired in a minute. No sir, Bill. If anything, I've got to treat your daughter like she carried the plague."

"She's not used to that. Men generally fall all over themselves to help her."

"Not me," Clint said. "Not if I want to stick around long enough to bring Sheriff Mintner down."

They were sitting at the edge of the boardwalk in front of Clint's little shop. Buttering twisted around and looked at the new window, the repaired door, and the sign he'd paid out of his own pocket that read: EXPERT GUNSMITHING.

"What about the shop?"

"Rent it out to someone else," Clint said. "Or use it as a storage room because your own is too small."

"Yeah," Buttering conceded. "I could do that. But I was hoping that you'd make a go of it here in Big Pine. That you'd prosper and maybe even . . ."

Clint shook his head. "Don't say it, Bill. Some things just aren't meant to be. I'm not meant to marry Angie and inherit your general store."

"Maybe you'd change your mind."

"Sorry, but being a storekeeper isn't my style."

"But working for a monster is?"

"I'll bring him down, Bill. You've got my word on it. It's the only way I can get to the man. Trust me."

"All right," Buttering said, not sounding very happy. "But I don't like it a damn bit."

"Neither do I," Clint said, "but I can't sit here and rot waiting for customers, and there's a woman that I was very fond of that is buried in your town cemetery. Her death demands justice, and I can't leave until justice is done."

"I understand," Buttering said. Then he climbed heavily to his feet and went back to work, leaving Clint to enjoy the last rays of the setting sun.

THIRTEEN

Clint checked his six-gun, took a deep breath, and then stepped into the sheriff's office. "Howdy," he said with a cheerfulness that belied the tension he felt inside. "Got a good game goin', huh?"

Sheriff Mintner and Deputy Bogard looked up from the cards they were holding. They were playing for matchsticks, and Mintner had obviously been winning. At the sight of the Gunsmith, the sheriff laid his cards down and came to his feet. Bob Bogard did the same.

"Hello, Clint," the sheriff said. "Are you here on business or pleasure?"

"Business. I'm here to accept your offer of becoming your number one deputy."

Bogard's head snapped toward Mintner, and he exclaimed, "You offered *him* a job?"

"I did," the sheriff said.

"But what about me?"

The sheriff heaved a big sigh. "I'm afraid that you'll have to turn in your badge. You see, the Gunsmith is worth a lot more to me than you are."

Bogard paled. His initial shock quickly turned to outrage. Bogard's lip curled, and he said, "Goddamn you,

Sheriff, I deserve a hell of a lot better than this! I been working for you over a year."

"Nothing lasts forever," Mintner said quietly.

"Yeah!" Bogard whirled on the sheriff. He was a tall man, wiry, and filled with rage. "If you fire me, that isn't going to be the end of it by a damn sight!"

"What does that mean?"

"It means I could raise a hell of a lot of trouble for you."

Mintner's slight grin dissolved. He reached into his desk drawer, found a badge, and tossed it to Clint. "Deputy Adams, why don't you take a little walk around town just to make sure that everything is under control?"

"I think everything is fine," Clint said, his eyes shifting back and forth between Mintner and Bogard as he sought to gauge what was going on. "Seems to me that the real trouble is right here, among us."

"Which I prefer to handle in private," the sheriff said.

Clint could see that he really had no choice but to do as he was told if he wanted to work for Big Al Mintner. He dipped his chin and headed back out the door, almost colliding with Miss Angie Buttering.

"What were *you* doing in there?"

Clint grinned, buffed his new badge on his shirt, and then pinned it in place. "I'm the new town deputy," he said, knowing that she would not be pleased.

"You're *what*?"

"I've just been deputized."

"That's . . . that's impossible!"

"Afraid not," Clint said. "You could ask the sheriff, but I think he's kind of preoccupied at the moment. Want to accompany me on my first rounds?"

"I don't believe this," she said, pushing past him into the sheriff's office.

"Angie, you come back later!" Mintner shouted. "I'm busy!"

Angie backed out of the sheriff's office, her face flushed with either anger or embarrassment. Shooting Clint a look that would kill, she stomped off down the boardwalk, her caboose sashaying back and forth just as proud and pretty as the butt end of a peacock.

"Hey wait!" Clint called, hurrying after her. "As long as we're both going in the same direction, we might as well get better acquainted."

"I don't want to get acquainted with you!"

"Aw, sure you do," Clint said, taking her arm. When Angie tried to pull free, Clint held her tight.

"Let go of me!"

"You're so pretty, you need my protection," Clint said, letting go anyway.

"I don't like you, and I can't imagine why Allen deputized you in the first place, but you can bet I'll find out!"

Angie was marching down the boardwalk, and Clint had to stretch his legs just to keep up with her. "Thing of it is," he said, "the sheriff just came to his senses."

"Says you!"

"It's a fact," Clint said, matching her stride for stride. "The sheriff recognizes that one good man is worth three bad ones—which is what he had on the payroll."

"You sure think highly of yourself, don't you?"

"I have my limitations," Clint conceded.

"Well, they don't include modesty."

Clint had to laugh at that, which seemed to make Angie even angrier. She almost knocked down two older women who were exiting a millinery shop and didn't even bother to say, "I'm sorry."

"You shouldn't get so worked up about things," Clint said, pursuing her to the end of the street. "It's not good for your heart."

"My heart is just fine, thank you!"

Angie kept walking. Past the Hurleys' livery and on up the road. Clint stuck with her. "Where are we going?"

"I'm going to . . . to walk. And I'd appreciate it if you'd just leave me alone!"

"Well, ma'am," he said, "I would, except that I'm the new deputy, and I think that Sheriff Mintner would prefer that I keep an eye out for your safety. There's some pretty rough customers around these parts, and you're an awfully pretty girl. Too pretty to be so upset and to be out walking by yourself along the road."

Angie Buttering stopped and whirled. She took a swing at the Gunsmith, but he jumped back with a grin. "Miss Buttering, you sure do show your appreciation in a strange way."

"You . . . you're awful! I'll get you fired, you idiot!"

"Whew," Clint said, "you really *are* upset."

"What about all the material and money my father gave you to fix up that shop?"

"It's still his to rent to someone else."

"Did you tell him that you were going to give up so quickly?"

"Yep. And I even told him that I was going to go to work for the sheriff and find out who killed Sarah Taylor."

At the mention of the murdered woman's name, the anger drained out of Angie. "So," she said, "*that's* why you've pinned on that badge and why Allen has hired you."

"That's right. And I suppose he has other reasons."

"Such as?"

"I don't know yet," Clint admitted. "But I'll find out."

"Allen has made a terrible mistake by hiring you," Angie said. "One he'll live to regret."

Clint could have said that he wholeheartedly hoped so, but instead he just smiled. "Are we going to walk any farther, or are you ready to go back into town?"

Angie turned and looked back at the town, thought about it for a minute, then continued walking. Clint followed, but now a half step behind. It was a nice day, and he was enjoying strolling along after Angie, watching her cute little bustle rustle.

As if she could feel his eyes on her backside, Angie stopped and whirled. "You are staring at my behind! Aren't you?"

"I am. And it's lovely."

She had started to counter an expected denial, but now she was caught off guard and at a loss for words. "I . . . I find you exasperating," she finally said. "And your face is quite a mess."

Clint gingerly touched his black eye. "Deputy Wild and I had a slight disagreement a few days back. I'm told he's on his way to the doctor in Santa Fe."

"You must have hurt him very badly," Angie said with a frown.

"That was my sincere intention."

Angie stared at him. "I'm surprised, given your reputation as a quick-gun artist, that you didn't just shoot him to death."

"Probably should have."

Angie reached up and touched Clint's eye. "That's kind of nasty. Does it hurt very badly?"

"It still smarts," Clint said.

"There's a little stream across that meadow. I heard that the Indians used cold moss to reduce the pain and swelling."

"I heard that, too," Clint lied, "so why don't we find some cold moss?"

"All right," Angie said, lifting her skirts and taking off across the meadow.

They had to fight their way through thickets and willows to get to the stream, but it was worth it. The water was clear and cold, and there were deep pools where big trout lay like dark arrows along the bottom rocks. Angie removed her shoes and cooled her feet as she searched for moss.

"Here's some," she called to Clint who had eyes for nothing but the girl.

"Well, come here!" she said with a hint of exasperation.

Clint went over to her and remained motionless while she raised a handful of dripping moss, then slapped it against his eye.

"Ouch!"

"Sorry."

"Take it easy," he said, feeling water drip down his face and off his chin.

"Does it feel better?"

She was pressing the moss to his face, and her head was tilted back so that he could see the soft, warm hollow of her throat, see her pulse throb, and smell her hair. And though he knew that she was a conniving little witch, Clint could not resist putting his hands around her narrow waist and drawing her body close.

"What are you doing?"

He reached up, tore the dripping moss away, and flung it into the stream as he kissed her.

"Let go of me!"

She struggled in his arms only a moment and then she yielded to his kiss, pressing herself close to his body.

Her tongue found his, and her fingernails scratched softly against his back. When her hand dropped to his buttocks and her hips pushed against his own, the Gunsmith knew that he was lost. Like this woman or not, she was physically irresistible. Clint picked her up and carried her to the side of the stream.

They fell in a pile on the soft earth, and he grunted with pain from his battle wounds.

"You poor, battered thing," she whispered, her breath hot in his ear.

"Yeah, almost an invalid," he said, hands slipping down to pull up her dress. She helped by lifting her hips, and his fingers quickly sorted through her underclothing until they came to rest in the warm, wet place that made her squirm and moan.

"So," he said, his finger moving in and out of her, "you think that the sheriff has made a big mistake hiring me, do you?"

"Yes, oh yes," she breathed, her own hands working frantically to unbutton his pants and release his stiffening manhood.

"And I suppose that you'll tell him he should fire me for making love to his fiancée?"

"Yes. I mean, no!" Her eyes had been closed, but now they opened, wide with alarm. "You wouldn't dare . . ."

"No," Clint promised with a smile as he removed his cartridge belt, gun and holster, then helped her loosen his pants. "That wouldn't be very smart for either of us, would it?"

"He'd kill us both," Angie whispered. "If he ever suspected that you were alone with me, he'd go crazy."

"Then we'll have to come up with some story. But right now, I think he has his own hands full, poor man."

Angie crushed her lips to his, and when she finally freed his stiff rod from the confines of his clothing, she pulled on it with great urgency. "Come on!" she begged. "Hurry!"

Clint didn't need urging. He tore Angie's underclothing away and fell upon her like a starving beast. His long rod plunged into her soft wetness, and he felt her grab his buttocks and rake them with her fingernails, as if he didn't already have enough bruises and scratches.

Their union was not a thing of grace or beauty, but then neither of them intended it to be so. Plunging and bucking, gasping and panting, they went at each other with a passion that was not quenched until Angie threw back her head and would have screamed with pleasure if Clint had not covered her mouth with his own.

He felt her entire body stiffen, and then he drove himself deeper yet into her. Over and over his hips slammed into hers as he released his seed.

Spent at last, he rolled off of the beautiful girl and regarded her thoughtfully. "I never expected this," he said after a few minutes.

"Me neither. I guess you must think I'm pretty loose, huh?"

"What I think isn't important. It's what your father thinks that concerns me. And he thinks you are heading for a bad, bad fall."

Angie sat up and pulled on her underclothing. She smoothed her dress and said, "My father wouldn't be in business today—maybe wouldn't even be alive—if it wasn't for Allen's protection."

"And that's your excuse for sleeping with a man like that?"

Angie's cheeks burned red. "I don't need an excuse! We're getting married."

"I see."

She jumped to her feet. "I don't think you see anything."

He stood and buckled on his cartridge belt and holster. "I see that Allen Mintner is power mad. I don't know if he knows who murdered Sarah Taylor, but I'm sure that he's as crooked as a hound's hind leg. He's ruthless, Angie. If you married a man like that, sooner or later he'd be the death of you."

Her eyes flashed. "He's the most powerful man in the county, and he'll be the governor of New Mexico someday. And I'll be second to none."

"I see. And what about your father?"

"He'll be proud."

"Uh-uh," Clint said. "Your father will be turning over in his grave. Angie, he despises the man. It's killing him inside to see you wasting yourself on someone like Allen Mintner."

"The next thing that you're going to tell me is that I should fall in love with some poor hick that owns a little two-bit business and raise kids and go to church."

"No," Clint said, "I'm not telling you anything except that Mintner will take you down with him. I think you can do better, and I know your father deserves better. You're all that he has in this world, Angie."

Tears sprang into her eyes. "I'm taking care of him— and me! I know what I'm doing!"

"Sure you do," he said, "and—"

They both jerked around to peer through the trees toward Big Pine. "Those were gunshots," Clint said, starting back through the brush.

"It must be Allen and Deputy Bogard!" she cried, scrambling to catch up with him and, at the same time, brush the dirt and twigs from her clothes.

"I don't know," Clint said, hearing the ominous staccato of more gunfire, "but my guess is that Bob Bogard didn't hand over his badge without an argument."

Angie didn't say a word as they ran toward town.

FOURTEEN

When Clint and Angie reached the main street of Big Pine, there was a large, excited crowd gathered outside the sheriff's office.

"Oh no!" Angie cried, rushing into the crowd.

"Let us through!" Clint ordered, grabbing men and shoving them aside. "Let us through!"

When they finally managed to reach the sheriff's door, they saw the town doctor kneeling over Big Al Mintner. Angie rushed forward, sobbing. Clint saw Bob Bogard lying wounded in one corner. Men were trying to lift and transport him outside.

Going to the sheriff's side, Clint knelt beside the fallen man and said, "What happened?"

"He drew his gun on me when I asked for his badge," Mintner gritted. "I didn't want it to turn out this way. Should have asked you to stay."

"Yeah," Clint said. He turned to the doctor. "How is he?"

"He'll recover, but I'm not sure about Bogard. He's taken a bullet through the gut. I'm afraid he's come to a bad end."

Clint went over to Bob Bogard, who was gray-faced

with pain and approaching death. The man looked up at Clint and hissed, "You son of a bitch! If you hadn't come . . ."

"Easy," Clint said. He looked up at the men. "You boys go on outside. The doctor is here, and there's no need to move Bogard and cause him more pain than he's already suffering."

"But . . ."

"Out!" Clint ordered. "Everyone but the doctor—outside!"

The men didn't like it, but Clint's badge was evidence of his authority and they had little choice but to follow his orders. Once they were all outside, Clint went back and knelt beside the dying Bob Bogard.

"You're a goner anyway. Why don't you tell me who killed Sarah Taylor?"

"Go . . . to . . . hell!"

"You're going to get there first," Clint said. "Might as well ease your burden and conscience before leaving this world."

"I . . ." Bogard struggled to say, "I didn't kill her!"

"But you raped her. Who did murder her?"

Tears ran from the ex-deputy's eyes. "I don't know," he whispered. "I don't know!"

Clint's temper flared. "Damn it, you must know something! Have heard something! Who besides Jim Wild carries a bowie knife around?"

Bogard's eyes widened, and a cold smile tugged at the corners of his thin lips. "I . . . I guess that's for you to find out, ain't it, *Deputy*?"

Clint pushed to his feet knowing that he wasn't going to get anything out of this dying man, who displayed no conscience or remorse. Of the three deputies that had worked for Sheriff Mintner, now only one was alive, and that was Jim Wild, who wasn't Sarah's killer either.

Dead end.

The Gunsmith rubbed a hand across his face. If it hadn't been for Sarah's death, he'd have tossed his badge on the sheriff's desk, ridden out of Big Pine, and never looked back. This town was rotten to the core, and there was still a killer on the loose whose trail was getting colder by the day.

"Clint!"

The Gunsmith went over to kneel by the sheriff's side. Mintner grabbed his sleeve. "I'm not going to be able to fulfill my duty here for a few weeks. I expect you to uphold the responsibilities of this office."

"Count on it," Clint said, knowing Mintner was playing a role for the doctor and Angie.

"We've got to get Sheriff Mintner over to my office," the doctor said. "There's still a bullet lodged in his side. I'll have to dig it out and patch him up."

"I'll get some men to help," Clint said, going to the door and calling for volunteers.

When the people outside found out that Clint was asking for men to carry Big Al, most of them walked away.

"Someone find us a door or a wide plank to lay the sheriff on so we can carry him," Clint ordered.

"Take it easy, you brutes!" Angie cried a few minutes later as her fiancé was hoisted onto what had been serving as an outhouse door. "Can't you see he's hurt?"

The sheriff gritted his teeth and put the matter a little more bluntly. "You clumsy bastards are all going to pay if you jar me like that again!"

"Just relax," the doctor said, mopping his perspiring brow. "Sheriff Mintner, everything is going to turn out fine. Your wound is superficial. The bullet is lodged in muscle, I think."

"What do you mean, you *think*? Is it or not?"

"It may have passed through," the doctor said meekly. "I won't be able to tell until I've gotten you to my office and really cleaned the wound properly. But either way, you'll be just fine."

"The hell I will! I'm in pain. I need morphine, not sympathy! Morphine, you quack!"

"I gave all that I had to Deputy Bogard," the doctor explained. "His wound is fatal, and he's in agony. I'm sure—"

"You gave *all* of your morphine to that worthless son of a bitch?"

"Honey," Angie pleaded. "Don't upset yourself!"

"But I'm in pain, damn it!" Mintner raged. "And I need something for it right now!"

"Well, I'm sorry," the doctor said, not sounding at all sympathetic. "We can send someone out tonight. He could reach Santa Fe and be back in a day or two."

Mintner grabbed the doctor's arm, and his fingers dug into the man's flesh. "What have you got for me right now?"

"Whiskey," the doctor said, tearing himself loose. "I'm afraid that is all I have right now."

"Then get it!"

The doctor left in a huff as Angie tried to console her fiancé. For his own part, Clint turned his head and suppressed a half smile. He didn't envy the poor doctor in the slightest. Mintner was going to be a terrible patient. He waited until the man had been removed from the office, and then he returned to Bob Bogard, who was dying hard.

"You got any relatives I should let know you died?" he asked the young man.

Bogard's eyelids fluttered. He rolled his head sideways

to look at Clint, but the Gunsmith knew that the dying man couldn't really see him clearly. Bogard's eyes were already starting to glaze.

"I got . . . a sister. Name is Esther. She lives in . . . Denver."

"Married?"

"Yeah."

"Last name?"

Bogard swallowed. His hand snaked out to grab the Gunsmith's wrist. "Mintner got the drop on me," he whispered. "We was arguing and he . . . he just went for his gun and drilled me!"

"I figured as much," Clint said. "So he gunned you down in cold blood. Is that how it happened?"

Bogard's chin dipped. He was breathing hard and bathed in sweat. "I wish I was dead already! I surely do!"

"Your wish will be granted in a few minutes," Clint told the man. "And I hope that you are sorry for what you've done."

"I'm sorry I ever saw this goddamn town!" Bogard sobbed.

"That makes two of us. And I'm sorry I haven't a clue as to who murdered Sarah Taylor."

"He was a big man. Saw him run off. Big footprints in the dust and . . . oh, sweet Jesus!" Bogard cried a moment before he went limp.

The Gunsmith shook his head, looking at the dead man for a minute. Then he went through Bogard's pockets, hoping for some clue or bit of insight into the man's past or Sarah's death. He found neither. Only a few dollars, which he confiscated for his own benefit because no one in this miserable town had a more desperate need for money than himself.

"Well," the Gunsmith said, "at least the mortician will

be happy with the way things turned out today."

He dragged the body outside onto the boardwalk, and a crowd instantly materialized to gawk and make a big fuss.

"Someone get the mortician to cart this man off," Clint ordered. "And as of right now, I'm the acting sheriff! I want everyone to go about their business as usual. And if you don't have any business, then go home!"

The people of Big Pine didn't much like being ordered about like that, but they knew the Gunsmith wasn't one to argue with and that he'd been deputized by Sheriff Mintner. So they dispersed, and in less than half an hour, the mortician arrived in a buggy. The man jumped down from his hearse, collected the body, and drove off with it, not once meeting Clint's gaze.

"Clint?"

He turned to see Angie. She looked pale and upset, which was not in the least bit surprising. "Hello, Angie," he said. "You look like you could use a drink."

"I could," she said. "Allen is not taking this well. He said some terrible things to me."

Tears welled up in Angie's blue eyes, and it was all that Clint could do to resist taking her into his arms and giving her comfort. But there were a lot of townspeople watching and, if he did such a thing, the word would get back to Mintner and there would be hell to pay.

"Come on into the office," Clint said. "We can talk, and it'll just look like I'm being official."

Angie allowed herself to be ushered inside the office. Clint closed the door, and the young woman threw herself into his arms and began to cry.

"Angie," Clint said gently. "Get ahold of yourself. You're never going to get the richest man in this county to the altar if you don't get a grip on yourself."

She sniffled and looked up at him. "I know. And I mean to marry him, Clint! I really do."

"Why?" he asked impulsively. "Is his money and power so important that they're worth selling your soul for?"

"No," she said quickly. "I . . . you think you know Allen, but you really don't. He's got some good in him along with the bad."

"He gunned down his deputy, Angie. Shot him down before he could react."

"He wouldn't do that!"

"Bob Bogard is winging his way to hell. But if he were here, he'd tell it's true."

Angie shook her head. She clamped her hands over her ears, and then she broke away from the Gunsmith and raced for the door.

FIFTEEN

Clint checked out of his hotel room and moved his belongings over to the sheriff's office. There was a set of bunk beds which had been used by the deputies in addition to a locker where he could store his saddlebags and extra clothing. He didn't have much privacy, and there would be even less when he had a prisoner or two in the small iron cells at the rear of the office. But money was tight, and Clint figured that he ought to be available to the people of Big Pine on a full-time basis while he took Sheriff Mintner's place during the man's brief convalescence.

After a big breakfast, Clint spent the entire morning cleaning out the sheriff's office. He swept the floors, dusted off the cabinets, and generally straightened things up. He couldn't help thinking of Sarah when he dusted. He inspected the few rifles and shotguns that were posted in the rifle rack and found them to be outdated relics.

"Hello in there!"

Clint turned to see Bill Buttering standing in the doorway. "Come on in," he said.

Buttering hobbled inside, looked around, and said, "I haven't set a foot in here since Mintner took office, but I wanted to give you a warm welcome. I think you'll find that other citizens will stop by as well."

"The door is open." Clint smiled wryly. "When I was trying to get my gunsmithing business off the ground, people treated me like I had a case of the bubonic plague. Now, you're telling me that they'll get friendly. This is a strange town, Bill."

"Not strange," the one-armed store owner corrected. "This is a town that has been cowed by Al Mintner for too long. I think that you're going to hear some very interesting stories once the people get accustomed to the idea that you're the law."

"But I'm not," Clint said, wanting to set the record straight right from the start. "I'm a *deputy*, Bill. I *work* for Al Mintner who is the sheriff. And I doubt that he'll be laid up more than a week. So you need to . . ."

Buttering shook his head. From out of his back pocket, he produced a sheet of paper. "I've got a petition here, and I'm going to fill it with enough signatures to hold a special town election next week."

"What for?"

"To elect you as permanent town sheriff and to get rid of Al Mintner."

"Now whoa up there, Bill!" Clint said, leaning his broom up against the wall and going over to the man. "I never said that I'd even accept the job."

"Why not?"

"Because I've been sheriff and marshal of towns for most of my adult life, and I'm retired."

Buttering's face dropped. "You can't just leave us in the lurch, Clint! With your help, we can clean the slate. Get Mintner to either quit controlling Big Pine or to move out. You're the only one that can do it. Don't walk out on us, Clint, you're our only hope."

Clint could see the pleading look in Bill Buttering's eyes and hear the desperation in the man's voice. He was touched, but also a realist. "Listen," he said, "word will get back to Mintner about this petition and there will be hell to pay. I'm guessing that he is going to be very, very unhappy with you, Bill."

"To hell with him! We either take a stand now, or I'm packing up everything in my store and moving to Santa Fe. I can't take watching this town grovel under Mintner any longer."

"And what about Angie?"

At the mention of his daughter, Buttering's face pinched with pain. "I can't take watching Angie throw her life away on such a man any longer either. If she wants to come, she's welcome. If not, then I'm leaving anyway if you won't agree to take office—at least until we can find an honest and capable replacement."

Clint's brow furrowed. He walked over to the front window and stared out into the street. Big Pine had been big trouble for him from the moment he'd arrived, but the Gunsmith could see that this had once been a fine place to live. The Gila River fed the valley with enough irrigation to produce a fine hay crop, and the soil was dark and yielded to the planting of crops. The town itself was appealing, and there were good families here trying to make their living and raise their kids to be solid citizens. But what chance did they have when the town was controlled by one unscrupulous man? No chance.

"Well?" Buttering said. "Are you going to allow me to fill this petition and hold a new election, or are you going to turn your back on us?"

"You're a very persuasive man," Clint said, turning to face his friend. "I tell you what. Give me a couple of days to think it over."

"Aw, come on! What—"

"Bill," Clint said, placing his hand on the Civil War veteran's thin shoulder, "I need a couple of days to try and dig up who murdered Sarah Taylor. After that, I'll let you circulate the petition. Deal?"

Buttering's chin dipped. "All right," he said, voice husky with emotion. "What do you need? Two days? Three?"

"Three," Clint said. "If I can't find any clues to the killer's identity in three days, then I'll just have to admit that the trail has gone stone-cold and the real killer might never be brought to justice."

"That'd be a hard thing to admit."

"Yeah," the Gunsmith said. "But with three days and a little luck, maybe something will break. Before he died, Bob Bogard said that the man who murdered Sarah was a big man with big feet."

"So? There are dozens of big men in this town."

"I know, but if Bogard saw the man, maybe someone else did, too. Besides, I found the murder weapon in the sheriff's desk. I'm going to take it around and ask everyone I see if they recognize that bowie. Someone *must* have seen it before. And then, if the man they finger is big, I'll have enough evidence to arrest him on suspicion of murder."

"It's that simple, huh?"

"It's not simple at all," Clint replied. "When I was asking questions before, I got stonewalled. Now that I'm a deputy and you're going to go around and introduce me to everyone, I think I can get people to talk."

Buttering smiled. "So, I help you and you'll help Big Pine. Is that it?"

"Yep."

"It's a deal!"

Clint grinned. "Good. Let's go get something to eat and then start talking to folks. I don't want to leave a stone unturned, and with this badge and your help, I feel that we just might strike pay dirt in the next few days."

The Gunsmith locked up the office and stepped outside. He glanced up and down the street, then turned to Buttering and said, "This is a real pretty little town."

"It is," the man agreed. "First time I saw it, I was struck by the beauty of the valley. I'd like to stay here rather than go to Santa Fe."

"Well," Clint said, as they started down the street, "we'll just see if lady luck finally turns her face and smiles on us. I want Sarah's murderer so bad that I can taste it."

"You don't give up on a thing very easily, do you?"

"No," Clint admitted, "but then, neither do you."

That comment brought a wide smile to Buttering's thin face as they stumped up the street.

After their meal, they began to make the rounds of businesses. It was slow work, but they were well received thanks to Buttering's introduction. They met first with Joe Baker, one of the town's civic leaders and owner of the local feed store.

"Joe," Buttering said, "I reckon you know Deputy Adams. He's taking the sheriff's place while he recovers. Terrible thing about Deputy Bogard."

"Damn bloody business it was," Joe said, removing his hat and wiping his bald pate. He was a stocky man in his early forties, grim and all business. "I've seen enough bloodshed in Big Pine to last the rest of my lifetime."

"So have I," Buttering replied, nodding his head vigorously. "But with Deputy Adams in charge now, things will change. And one of first orders of the deputy's business is to find out who murdered poor Sarah Taylor and bring that man to justice."

"Terrible thing that, too," Joe said, mopping his face of perspiration. "Must've been a low son of a bitch to kill a woman like Sarah. I liked her, even if the wife said she wasn't worth much."

"She was a good-hearted woman," Clint said. "And I am asking everyone if they have any idea who might have killed her."

"Afraid not."

Clint had the sheathed murder weapon pushed behind his belt, and now he brought it out for display. "Have you ever seen this knife before?"

Joe stared at it with morbid fascination. "That the one that was stuck in her?"

"It is." Clint extended the knife to Joe, who took a step back. "No thanks. I don't want to even touch the damned thing. I never seen it before."

"Who else carries a bowie knife like this?"

"Lots of men."

"Would you write down their names? You have my word I won't tell them where I got the information."

Joe cast a worried glance toward Bill Buttering. "Look," he said, "I told you I liked Sarah, but . . ."

"I've been a good friend to you, Joe. I've given you credit when you had no cash. Now, I'm asking you to help Deputy Adams find Sarah's killer."

"But what if it gets back to whoever did it that I gave a list to Adams?"

"He told you that wouldn't happen." Buttering's voice took on a reassuring tone. "Besides, we've already gotten a number of lists from other people in town."

"You have?"

"Yep. Yours will just be one of many."

"Well, in that case, sure."

A few minutes later, they were walking out of the feed store and Clint was stuffing the list into his shirt pocket. He glanced sideways at Bill Buttering and said, "You sure can tell a smooth story. Thanks."

"It's all right," the man assured him. "Besides, before three days have passed, you'll have a dozen such lists with the names of every man who has been in Big Pine wearing a bowie knife."

"Let's just hope that the murderer wore it in public," Clint, said, as they entered the town's weekly newspaper, the *Big Pine Gazette*.

By the end of that first day, thanks to Bill Buttering's help, Clint had twenty-two names, but many were duplicates. The next morning, they visited the last few businesses in town, one of which was the blacksmith's shop.

"Earl, this is Deputy Adams," Bill said. "I'd like you to give us a few minutes of your time while we explain what we're up to."

"I *know* what you're up to," Earl said. "You're collecting names of anyone who carries or has carried a bowie knife."

Earl was a large, shirtless man. He smelled like a sweaty horse, and his face was dark with soot. The palms of his hands were as big and hard as the horseshoes he forged. Now, he wiped those hands on his leather apron and said, "I got a real short list, but I ain't written it down 'cause I can't write."

"Then give me the names out loud," Clint said.

"Buck Simpson, Larry Jeeter, Amos Hollings, Jim Spense, Art Pate, Win Jackson, and Milt Frank."

"I already had all those names a bunch of times except one," Clint said. "Who is Win Jackson?"

"Elwin," Buttering said. "You remember his brother Dominic."

"Elwin is the mean drunk with one hand blown off, right?"

"That's right."

Clint frowned. "How come neither you nor anyone else has mentioned Elwin before?"

Buttering shrugged. "I don't know. I never saw him wearing a bowie knife. Are you sure you know what you're talking about?"

"Hell yes," the blacksmith said. "He don't wear it out in the open, but in a sheath under his shirt. Lots of men wear 'em hidden like that."

The blacksmith looked down at the murder weapon. "Elwin had a bowie like that. I saw it one time 'cause he asked me to straighten and sharpen it for him. He was using the damn thing to pry river rocks up looking for fish bait."

"Take a real close look at this knife," Clint ordered. "Is it the same one that you worked on?"

Earl took the knife, turned it in his big hand a time or two, and said, "I can't swear by it, because it was three or four years ago that I worked on Elwin's bowie. And these knives are pretty damn common."

"Look closer. Give me your best guess," Clint said, almost pleading.

Earl frowned. "Light in here is poor. Let's step outside."

Outside, the blacksmith turned the knife to the sun, one way and then the other. "Yep," he said, "this is the one."

"Are you sure?"

"Yep. Look. See the little cuts made from my vise grip? I've sharpened hundreds of bowie knives, and I do 'em all the same. I can tell 'em even after a long time. I sharpened this knife, and when I did, it belonged to Win Jackson."

Clint expelled a deep breath.

"You got him," Bill Buttering whispered.

"Maybe."

"What do you mean, *maybe*?"

"He might have lost or sold the knife. Someone might have taken it from him. All we know for sure is that he once owned the murder weapon."

"But Elwin wouldn't sell his knife!"

"Then maybe he lost it," Clint said. "I mean to find out one way or the other."

Clint turned to the blacksmith. "You might have just helped me to find Sarah's murderer. I appreciate your honesty, and I trust you'll testify in court to what you've just said."

"Now wait a damn minute!" Earl protested. "No one said anything about no court."

"You'd have to do it so that we could get a conviction," Clint said. "Your testimony would be—"

"I ain't givin' no testimony to nobody! Win Jackson is one mean son of a bitch! I don't want him to come lookin' for me!"

"You're a big, strong man," Clint said. "Are you saying you're afraid of Elwin?"

"Damn right I am! And you should be, too! He's a bad one. And even if I did whip him, he'd find a way to bring me down. Maybe a bullet in the back, or burning my shop down some night. I don't know, but he would!"

Clint sighed. He understood, but that did not help matters. "All right," he said, not wanting to upset the blacksmith any more until he decided Elwin was his man and had made his arrest. After Elwin was behind bars, perhaps the blacksmith would feel differently about being called in to testify before a court of law.

"Thanks," Buttering said.

"You don't tell Win about any of this, you hear me?"

"Sure," Buttering said as they left the blacksmith's shop.

Outside, Buttering grabbed Clint's arm. "Do you think Elwin murdered Sarah?"

"I don't know," he replied, "but I'm going to saddle my horse, ride out to his place, and find out."

"He's dangerous, and so is Dominic. I'll come with you."

"No," Clint said. "You've done enough already. This is what I'm best at, and I'm best alone. No offense, Bill, but I'll do better if I don't have to worry about you getting shot."

"Sure," Buttering said, looking crestfallen but also a little relieved. "You're the Gunsmith. I'm just a crippled old soldier who can't . . ."

"Don't say that," Clint said. "Why, at every business we've visited yesterday and today, *you* were the sole reason anyone cooperated. Without the respect these people have for you, I'd never have gotten in their doors."

"Is that right?"

"You know it is," Clint said, seeing the man's face take on a glow of pride. "It's clear to me, even if it isn't to you, that you are the most respected man in Big Pine. I'd say you ought to add your name to that petition you want to have passed around for signatures."

"My name?" Buttering didn't understand. "I couldn't be the sheriff!"

"I was talking about being the new mayor," Clint said, watching the storekeeper swell with pride.

He left Bill Buttering then and headed for the livery to claim Duke. It would feel good to be in the saddle again, even if he was riding into a double-edged buzz saw named Dominic and Elwin.

SIXTEEN

Before leaving town. Clint got plenty of advice and exact directions from Bill Buttering. "They live about a mile south of town along the Gila River. You'll see a thick stand of cottonwoods, and that's where they've built their place. I've never even been there, but other folks have told me it's just a ramshackle cabin."

"And I suppose that the country around that stand of trees is pretty open?"

"That's right. And them brothers got a couple of wolf dogs that are mean as badgers. I doubt that you'll get near the place without starting off a howl."

"Then there is no reason to attempt to gain the element of surprise," Clint said. "I might as well just ride in bold as brass and see what happens."

"What will happen is that Elwin will come out with a rifle and tell you to get the hell off his land!"

"I'll deal with that. What about Dominic? Will he also fight?"

"Not if he's sober. But if you have to draw down on Elwin . . . well, my guess is that you'd have to do the same with Dominic. Them two fight like dogs and cats, but they're tighter than paint on the wall."

Buttering fidgeted. "Are you sure that I can't go along? I may be one-armed and one-legged, but I can still hold a six-gun and generally hit what I aim for."

"Thanks, but no thanks," Clint said, heading for the livery to get his horse.

When he arrived at the Hurley livery, young Dan and his grandfather, Dud, were resting in the shade of the barn. The boy jumped up at the sight of the Gunsmith and said, "Mr. Adams! You sent for any of them famous lawmen friends of yours yet?"

"No," Clint said, "I haven't. They're pretty busy fellas, and we don't call on each other unless it's real important. Last time I saw Wild Bill Hickok, he was up to his neck in trouble, and Wyatt Earp is a hard man to run down."

The boy could not hide his disappointment. "But they'd come if you sent for 'em needing help, wouldn't they?"

"Why, sure they would!"

"I almost hope you do need help," Dan said.

"What I need right now is my horse saddled," Clint told the kid as he flipped him a quarter. "Suppose you can do that?"

"Why, sure!"

When the boy was gone, Clint took his chair and sat down beside the old man. He made idle conversation for a moment, then came to the point. "Have you ever been out to the Jackson place, Mr. Hurley?"

"Sure, a time or two when I had no choice," the old man said. "Is that where you're going?"

"It is."

"And I don't expect it's for a social call."

"You got that right." Clint: said. "I need to ask Elwin some questions about Miss Taylor's death."

"You think he killed her?"

"There's a good chance of it."

The old man scowled. "Don't seem possible to me. Elwin hates and avoids people, women most especially."

"Maybe he hated Miss Taylor enough to stab her."

"Maybe he did."

Clint thumbed the rim of his hat back. "Did Elwin or Dominic ever have anything to do with the ladies?"

"Elwin didn't. He wouldn't know what to do with his pecker other than to piss through it."

Clint closed his eyes for a minute. "Well, I tell you," he said, "it's the quiet ones that can fool you, Mr. Hurley. Elwin might just hunger for a woman. He might have gone to pay for Sarah, and she not only said no—she said *hell no*! Then he stabbed her."

"I suppose that sort of thing happens, huh?"

"All the time," Clint said. "In my years as a lawman, I've caught some of the most unlikely murderers. Sometimes men that you'd never expect harbor hatreds and vengeance that consume and drive them to murder."

"Elwin has a lot of hate in him—but so does Dominic."

"I met Dominic. He seems kind of . . ."

"Simple?"

"Yes."

"He is simple, just like his brother. But I heard that Dominic craves the flesh of loose women. He's gone to Santa Fe to spend the night with 'em more than a few times. He likes them Mexican girls, but I heard that most of 'em won't have a thing to do with him. I'll bet he has to pay double just to lie with the ugliest whores in all of Santa Fe."

"Dominic ever carry a bowie knife?"

"Nope. I seen him with an old broken Army Colt. Same one that blew out all the chambers and took his brother's hand clean off. He used to show it off to whoever would buy him a drink. He seemed to think it was real funny."

"They sound like quite a pair," Clint said. "I guess that Dominic works around town doing odd jobs, huh?"

"He does. The sheriff uses him and Elwin to paint and fix up some of his properties."

"Is that right?"

"Yep. Mintner is about the only one that will hire the crazy bastards."

"That doesn't seem too surprising. I wonder if . . ."

"Here's your horse!" Dan said, leading Duke out of the barn.

The Gunsmith smiled to see Duke and the way his coat shined. He gave the kid an extra two bits. "You're taking fine care of him, and I'm grateful, Dan."

The boy grinned. "I'd give anything to own this horse someday, Mr. Adams."

"Well, I'm afraid that he's going out to pasture about the same time that I am," Clint replied with a wink. He climbed into the saddle, and it felt good.

"You best have your carbine in your hands," the old man warned. "And if you don't see Elwin at first, then you'd better get out of rifle range because he'll potshot you for certain. And even one-armed, that sneaky bastard is a damned fine shot."

"Thanks for the warning."

"And if you see a big, spotted, black-and-white cur, shoot 'im on sight! The son of a bitch bit me the last time I was at the Jackson place. He snuck up quiet as a rat and took a hunk out of my leg like it was a piece of cheese. So you watch out for that dog and any others that come at you 'cause the whole pack of 'em are worse'n wolves!"

"I will," Clint said. "I kind of wish that I had a shotgun after what you've just told me."

"Give him mine, Dan. It's behind the door to my room. And give him some of those extra shells in my trunk."

"Yessir!"

Dan vanished into the huge barn for the shotgun. The old man waited a minute and then said, "If you get in trouble, you shoot the both of them brothers. You don't turn your back on 'em for a minute. Give 'em no chances. They're sneaky, and they're deadly. And if they think that you're looking to pin Sarah Taylor's murder on 'em, they'll try to take you out in a hail of bullets."

"I'll remember that."

When Dan returned, it was with a double-barreled, twelve-gauge shotgun that was in good working order and loaded with buckshot. Clint inspected the weapon and nodded his appreciation. He stuffed the extra shells in his shirt pockets.

"Think nothing of it, just shoot that spotted dog with the first load and use the second on Elwin."

"I will if I have to."

"You'll have to," Dud Hurley said with complete conviction.

The Gunsmith galloped out of town, armed to the teeth with a well-oiled six-gun, his saddle carbine, and the double-barreled shotgun cradled across his cantle. He could feel that Duke wanted to lay back his ears and run, so he let him for the first half mile. Then, when he saw the dense stand of cottonwoods beside the Gila River, he reined the horse to a walk.

At four hundred yards, the dogs saw him and came rushing out of the trees, barking and snarling. And right in the front of the pack was a big, black-and-white spotted animal with its long yellow fangs very much in evidence.

The Gunsmith raised the shotgun. He didn't especially want to open fire on the dogs, but he had Duke to think of first, and he wasn't about to have this pack of dogs hamstring his precious black gelding.

"Get back!" he shouted in warning.

But the dogs kept coming, and when they were fifty yards away and showed no signs of breaking off their attack, Clint threw the shotgun to his shoulder, took aim on the leader, and pulled the trigger.

The shotgun exploded buckshot that ripped into the leader along with several of those nearest. The black-and-white dog struck the ground rolling, and it was clear that he wasn't ever going to bite anything again. Several of the other dogs, also wounded, managed to veer away and went off howling into the trees. A second warning shot over the heads of the undecided made them turn tail and race off, howling in fear.

Clint reloaded from the box of shells that Dud Hurley had provided. He dismounted and walked over to the dog that had snuck up on Old Dud Hurley and bitten him so badly. The dog stared up at him in death, and Clint felt no remorse. A biting dog was far worse than a nuisance.

Good riddance.

The Gunsmith looked at the trees and shouted. "Dominic, it's me, Clint Adams! You remember that we talked? We need to talk again!"

Dominic Jackson appeared from the trees. "You shot the hell out of my dogs!" he screamed. "You kilt the best one and you wounded them others! Damn you to hell!"

"Dominic, I didn't want to shoot the dogs, but they were going to attack my horse! I tried to scare them off, but they wouldn't go. Now we need to talk!"

"No!"

"We either talk peacefully, or I'll come in and shoot you just like I shot your dog! And I want to talk to your brother as well. Sheriff Mintner has appointed me as his new deputy, and I have the right to ask questions. If you don't come out peacefully, then the sheriff will have me put you and your brother in jail!"

Dominic disappeared for a minute, and just when the Gunsmith was about to start forward, the man reappeared, hands held over his head. "I'm comin'!"

"Where's your brother, Elwin?"

"He's . . . he's gone huntin'."

"Like hell he has!"

Dominic trudged out, and when he came to what was left of his big black-and-white mongrel, he kicked it in anger. "Stupid son of a bitch!" he screamed. "Gettin' yourself shot like that for nothin'!"

"Come here," Clint said, keeping the shotgun loosely trained on the man. "Are you armed?"

"No, sir! I only got a broken Army Colt and an old broken Kentucky rifle. You see it was . . ."

"Never mind that," Clint said shortly. "Turn around."

"What are you going to do?"

"I've got a pair of handcuffs, and I'm going to use them on you."

"No!" Dominic cried, his face twisting in horror. "I . . . I ain't done nothing wrong!"

"Fine. Then you've got nothing to worry about. Now turn around."

But Dominic shook his head and lashed out with a boot at the Gunsmith's groin. It was all that Clint could do to sidestep the wicked kick and bring the barrel of his shotgun crashing down against the side of Dominic's skull. The big man collapsed in a heap.

Clint handcuffed Dominic's thick wrists behind his back, then tied his feet at the ankles. Satisfied that the man was out of this fight until its conclusion, Clint next turned his attention back to the thick stand of cottonwood trees, sure that Elwin was hiding with a rifle ready to take his life.

Clint's suspicion was confirmed an instant later when a bullet whistled past his head. The shot was close enough that Clint didn't wait around to see if the next one found its mark. Without shame or hesitation, he yanked off his Stetson and used it to bat Duke across the muzzle. The gelding went flying back toward Big Pine, and the Gunsmith dove for cover behind Dominic.

"You'll kill your own brother before you kill me!" he shouted as another bullet whistled by just inches from his head.

"To hell with him! I'll kill you both!"

Clint believed Elwin. And now, with his horse racing back to town, he had a tough decision to make. He could either remain behind the big, unconscious form of Dominic and allow the man to be killed, or he could jump up and sprint out of rifle range.

The Gunsmith decided that he did not want to have Dominic's death on his conscience so he jumped up and ran with bullets tracking him across the valley floor. And when the bullets stopped flying, Clint halted, bent over, and sucked in badly needed air.

After a few minutes, he felt revived and marched over to the river where he sat down to wait until nightfall. When darkness finally came, the Gunsmith checked his Colt and the shotgun, then circled the stand of cottonwood trees in order to come in from a fresh angle. He had no illusions about taking Elwin by surprise. The man's pack of dogs would insure that Elwin had plenty of warning. But at least Clint knew that he would be off the open land and in among the trees where he could have the same advantages that Elwin Jackson had claimed earlier.

Clint was tired and anxious as he gained the cotton-woods. He could hear Dominic shouting and cussing as he fought the handcuffs. Maybe Dominic's shouts would distract Elwin and the dogs at least long enough for Clint to get into a good firing position.

The half-moon overhead offered just a dim yellow light that failed to penetrate the overhanging canopy of cotton-wood leaves as Clint moved nearer to the cabin with the shotgun balanced in his fists. Where was Elwin? In the cabin, or more likely out in the trees waiting to ambush him? Clint put himself in Elwin's shoes and knew the man would be hiding in the trees.

All right, then, the Gunsmith thought. I'll find him.

He began moving from one tree to the next, making a rough circle around the cabin, sure that he would intercept Elwin and the dogs. He was right. Ten minutes later he saw all of them just up ahead. He was downwind of a slight breeze and that saved him from being detected by the dogs. Clint stepped out from the trees, raised his shotgun, and yelled, "Freeze, Elwin!"

The one-handed man whirled. Clint could see that he was massive and that the rifle in his fist looked like a mere toy. Elwin opened fire, dropped the rifle, and reached for the Colt on his hip. Clint saw the dogs rush him, and just before he leapt for a low-hanging branch, he fired both of the shotgun's barrels. It wasn't until he was safe on a thick limb with only his Colt revolver clenched in his fist that the Gunsmith realized that Elwin was down and the dogs, the ones that had survived this second blast of buckshot, were gone.

Clint dropped out of the tree and warily moved toward the still figure. "Elwin, are you dead?"

It was a dumb question, but at least it broke the ominous silence. When Clint reached the big man, he kicked him in the foot and there was no reaction. Keeping his six-gun trained on Elwin, he moved around him until the feeble light of the moon was directly on Elwin's face. And what a face it was! Clint grimaced to see how the exploding cylinders of an Army Colt had badly disfigured the huge man.

He crouched and then reached out to check to see if there was a carotid pulse at the base of Elwin's neck. Suddenly, the man grabbed Clint's wrist and bellowed insanely. Elwin Jackson was so powerful that he jerked Clint completely off his feet and so quick that he managed to get a headlock around Clint's neck and hug him.

Sheer panic flooded through the Gunsmith as he felt Elwin's other arm, the one without a hand, clamp around his ribs and start to crush them. Clint knew that his six-gun had been knocked aside and that there was no hope for escape. His fingers clawed for Sarah's murder weapon sheathed at his belt. He found the handle and, somehow, he managed to tear it free. With the bones in his ribs and his neck practically popping like corks, Clint stabbed Elwin with his own bowie knife. Stabbed him again and again as the man bellowed and tried to break his neck.

It was nip and tuck who was going to die first, but at last Elwin Jackson's immense power bled away and his stinking body went limp. Clint rolled off the dead man and buried his face in the grass, panting for air and still clenching the bloody knife.

He might have passed out except that he heard a strange, approaching noise. Pulling his wits together, Clint lifted his chin to see Dominic hopping through the trees toward the Jackson cabin.

"Hold it right there!" the Gunsmith shouted. "That's far enough."

Dominic tried to turn, lost his balance, and crashed to the ground. Clint hurled the bloody bowie aside, saw his own Colt, collected it, and limped over to Dominic. "Where the hell did you think you were going?"

But the man didn't answer. He was staring at the still form of his dead brother. "You killed him."

It was a statement, not even an accusation. "Yeah," Clint said. "It wasn't the way I wanted to do it, that's for sure. But he was about to break my neck, and there wasn't time to do anything but use his own knife. I'm sorry that it worked out this way. Did you know your brother killed Miss Taylor?"

Dominic didn't answer. He was in a state of shock. Clint didn't want to arrest the man, so he said, "Roll over on your belly, and I'll unlock the handcuffs."

"You going to hang me?" Dominic asked in strained whisper.

"No, I'm turning you loose so that you can bury your brother and get on with your life."

Dominic didn't seem to understand. No matter. Clint found his key to the handcuffs, unlocked them, and then wished he hadn't tossed the bowie into the dark shadows so that he could cut the ropes that bound Dominic's ankles.

"I guess you can get those knots loose or find a knife and cut 'em yourself," Clint said to the man. "I'm heading for town."

"Will they come for me?"

"No." Clint wished he could make the confused and mentally deficient man understand that his own life was not in jeopardy. "Listen, Dominic, everything is going to be all right."

"Maybe they'll want to hang me. I dunno. They don't like us. They don't like us at all. Only friend we ever had in Big Pine was Sheriff Mintner."

"What are you going to do now that your brother is dead?"

"I dunno."

"Maybe it would be better if you moved on," Clint said. "There are some nice places to live other than here in this valley."

"But it's where I live!"

"Yeah, I know, but you might want to move on. People do that, Dominic. They do it all the time. Sometimes pulling up roots is the best thing when a place goes bad."

Dominic didn't seem to understand. He just kept staring at his brother's body, then casting his eyes over to the dead dog. Finally, he mumbled, "I don't want to hang."

"You *won't* hang," Clint told him. "I swear I'll tell everyone in town that you had nothing to do with Sarah Taylor's death. It'll be all right, Dominic. Everything passes with time. With you, I think it will pass in a hurry."

Clint wiped his bloody hands on his pants. "Now, do you want your brother buried here or in the town's regular cemetery?"

When Dominic didn't answer, the Gunsmith took that to mean that Dominic would bury his brother under the cottonwoods. That was fine with Clint.

All he wanted was to leave this dark place of death.

SEVENTEEN

It was only a mile back to Big Pine that night, but it was one of the longer walks of the Gunsmith's life. His ribs were bruised, his neck felt broken, and he knew that it would be so stiff in the morning that he would hardly be able to turn his head. But at least Sarah's killer had paid his dues. If he hadn't promised Bill Buttering that he'd stay in Big Pine until after an election that would depose Sheriff Mintner, the Gunsmith would have left this part of the country within the hour.

As he neared town, he realized that a large crowd was waiting for him. Clint wiped off his clothes and hoped that they did not see the bloodstains that covered his shirt and pants.

"Mr. Adams?"

Clint saw Angie and her father detach themselves from the anxious crowd and hurry forward.

Angie said, "Everyone heard shots. Are they . . . "

"Elwin is dead," Clint said, loud enough for the people to hear. "He's the one that murdered Sarah Taylor. But his brother, Dominic, didn't have anything to do with it. So I don't want anyone to bother the man. He's got a brother to bury, and he's confused enough as things stand. Is that understood?"

The crowd of silhouettes nodded with understanding. Bill Buttering took Dud Hurley's shotgun from Clint's hands. "I don't think you'll be needing this anytime soon."

"I hope not," Clint said. "Give it back to Dud with my thanks. Without that shotgun, I wouldn't have had a chance against Elwin and his damned dogs."

"Did you kill some dogs?"

"Yeah," Clint said, not wishing to elaborate. "It was them or me."

"That will please old Dud," Buttering said. "Now let's get you a bath and some new clothes. You look like you just fought Satan himself."

"Yeah, I feel like I have," Clint said. "And that Satan won."

Angie took his arm. "Allen wants to see you tonight."

"Tonight?" Clint asked.

"Yes."

Buttering scoffed. "He can damn sure wait until tomorrow morning!"

"I think you'd better see him as soon as you've cleaned up," Angie said, ignoring her father's outburst.

Something in her voice stopped Clint in his tracks and made him say, "All right. You go tell him I'll be along as soon as I've bathed and changed my clothes."

She managed a tight smile. "I'll do that. Please don't make him wait too long, Clint."

"Damn it!" Buttering stormed. "He can wait until hell freezes over!"

But Clint, ignoring the outburst said, "I'll be along in about an hour."

When Angie rushed off to tell Mintner of Clint's impending arrival, her father had a few more choice words. "You tell Mintner that *you* are the one that brought Sarah Taylor's murderer to justice and that *you* are the one who is going to be elected the next sheriff of Big Pine."

"I don't think that would be such a good idea," Clint said. "Why don't I just sort of test the waters and find out what Mintner wants? Don't you think that makes better sense? No reason to tip him off about our plans until necessary. The moment we do, he's going to come storming back into office and try to send me packing."

"Let him try! Let him just try! The people of this town will stand behind you if he tries to use that badge."

Clint wondered. He was sure that Bill Buttering would gladly die if he could kill Al Mintner in the process. But the other citizens of this town were of a different mind and heart. They'd been bullied for years, and Clint knew that they couldn't be counted upon to rally to his aid in an emergency.

Keeping that thought in mind, he let Bill take him to his own home where he bathed and some clean clothing was found. When Clint was dressed and his hair combed, he placed his black Stetson on his head and said, "What time is it?"

"Ten after midnight."

"I guess I'd better go see what Mintner has on his mind. Have you seen any new gunnies ride into town today?"

"No." Buttering's eyes widened. "Are you thinking that . . . "

"I don't know what to think," Clint said. "I just like to run the possibilities over in my mind before I step into the game."

"Sure."

Clint left the worried storekeeper and went to see Sheriff Allen Mintner. On the way, he checked his Colt to make sure that it was resting easy in his holster. He was damned glad that Elwin Jackson hadn't inflicted as much damage on his gun hand as he had on his poor ribs and neck.

Although Clint had previously been inside the Minter Mansion, as it was referred to in town, he'd entered through the back door. Now, coming in the front, he saw that the place had a circular gravel driveway and a portico with thick alabaster pillars. When Clint walked up the driveway, he saw that the front door to the mansion was wide open and every lamp in the place, upstairs and down, seemed to have been lit. The Mintner Mansion glowed like moonlight.

Angie rushed outside to intercept him. She looked very upset, and her cheeks were streaked with tears. "I'm not sure that it's such a good idea to go and see him now. Maybe you'd better—"

"I'll see him now," Clint said. "I've gone to considerable trouble to come over here tonight, and I'm not going to have this meeting hanging over my head. Where is he?"

"Upstairs in his bedroom. He's been drinking, and he's in a very nasty frame of mind."

"Does he know about your father's petition?"

"I'm not sure. Maybe."

"Did you tell him about Elwin Jackson?"

"Of course."

"All right, then. Why don't you stay downstairs while I have a talk with the emperor of Big Pine," Clint quipped. "One other thing, is he holding a hide-out gun under those covers or up his sleeve?"

Angie swallowed.

"Well?"

"Yes! But please don't shoot him! He's hurt, and he's been drinking. He's not himself tonight. If you'd just go away, I know he'd be much more agreeable in the morning."

"No thanks," the Gunsmith said, pushing past her into the house. He mounted a circular stairway, and when he came to the upstairs landing he paused.

"Is that you, Angie?" Mintner called. "Where is Adams, that back-stabbing son of a bitch! I told you to bring him here!"

Clint followed the voice. "I *am* here," he said, stepping into the rich man's bedroom.

"You," Mintner cried, stabbing an accusing finger in Clint's direction. "You went out to the Jackson place and you killed Elwin!"

"He murdered Sarah Taylor."

"Impossible!"

Clint took a backward step. "What do you mean?"

"I mean that he was here at the house the night that Sarah was killed. He was painting this house and fell from a ladder. He was stunned. I thought he'd broken his back and sent for the doctor. Elwin was badly bruised and laid up for two solid days before he could limp back to his own cabin."

"No."

"Yes!" Mintner's lips twisted in derision. "Ask the doctor if you don't believe me! Ask my men, they'll all tell you that there is no way that Elwin could have killed Sarah Taylor."

"But . . ."

"What kind of a professional are you anyway?" Mintner asked with a sneer. "You go out and stab an innocent man to death!"

Clint felt his reserves leak away. He knew in his very bones that Mintner wasn't lying. There was too much honest rage in the man.

"I went out to question Elwin Jackson, not kill him. He opened fire on me, not the other way around. It was self-defense. As a lawman, I had every right to ask that man questions."

"Elwin wasn't a man to ask anything! And he absolutely *hated* all women!"

Clint spotted a decanter of brandy and some glasses. He didn't ask Mintner if it would be all right to help himself to a big drink. When he'd tossed it down, he refilled his glass. He stared out the window and then said, "So I'm back to the beginning."

"No! You're fired."

Clint smiled, but there was no warmth in his voice when he unpinned his badge and said, "All right."

Mintner was caught off guard by the Gunsmith. He'd expected an argument. When Clint threw his badge on the bed, Mintner took it and said, "I'll expect you to be out of this town come daylight."

"Not a chance," Clint said. "I'm staying in Big Pine at least until after the election."

"What election?" Mintner asked with genuine surprise.

"The one that they're having in a couple of days to elect me the new sheriff," Clint said matter-of-factly.

Mintner blanched. "You've betrayed me!"

"I just gave in to an honest request to help free Big Pine from your corruption," Clint said. "You may own most of the downtown businesses, but Big Pine isn't your private kingdom, and you're not the judge, jury, and grand executioner anymore. In fact, when I'm elected and you're out of office, I'll make damn sure that you follow the exact letter of the law."

"You traitorous bastard!" Mintner shouted, hand moving under the covers.

Clint's gun hand flashed to his Colt, and it came out

in a smooth blur to point at Mintner. "I don't think that I'd do that," he warned. "I killed Elwin with a knife as he was about to snap my neck. Now with you, I'll take my time and put the first bullet where you least expect."

Mintner started to say something, then seemed to change his mind when he realized that Clint's Colt was aimed at his crotch. The rich man paled and yanked his hands out from under the covers. "Don't shoot! I'm already wounded!"

"Hell, up to now you've just been bullet-tickled," Clint scoffed. "I'm talking about putting a bullet in you where it will change your whole life. Make you giggle like a girl and wiggle like a woman. I'd be doing Miss Buttering the biggest favor of her pretty young life."

"Please," the man begged. "Don't shoot!"

Clint was in pain and out on his feet. He regarded Mintner with contempt and then turned his back and left the man cringing in his bed.

"Wait! Goddamn it, you come back here right now!"

But the Gunsmith wasn't listening. Instead, he hurried down the stairs and out into the sweet summer air. He felt empty and confused. If Elwin had not killed Sarah then . . .

"Dominic," he breathed, angling back out toward the distant stand of cottonwoods. "Dominic is the one that hungers for the whores! He's the one that murdered Sarah, not Elwin!"

Clint broke into a run.

EIGHTEEN

When the Gunsmith reached the stand of cottonwood trees that hid the Jackson cabin, he sat down and waited until he had his breath and his heartbeat slowed to normal. He could see the cabin, but there was no sign that it was occupied. The interior was dark and still.

Clint wondered about the dogs. There should have been a lot of them about, and this time he did not have the benefit of Dud Hurley's shotgun if the pack charged and tried to tear him to pieces. So what was he going to do?

After about a half hour of thinking on it, Clint decided to do nothing until first light, which was only a few hours away. With dawn, he'd be able to see the dogs and probably avoid having to kill Dominic. Having reached that decision, the Gunsmith climbed up into the crotch of a tree and rested secure with the knowledge that he would not be attacked in his sleep by the dogs, who were plenty capable of ripping out his throat.

He dozed fitfully and would have fallen except that he rigged his cartridge belt around a branch so that, whenever he started to fall asleep and lean too far to one side, the belt would catch him before he tumbled to the ground below. It was a hard three or four hours, and he was grateful when the sun finally burned an orange streak across the eastern horizon.

As the light strengthened, Clint decided to wait a little longer in his perch. With luck, Dominic would come out, and the Gunsmith figured he could then catch the man by surprise.

Another hour passed, and Clint began to get impatient when nothing stirred inside the cabin. He could see the fresh mound of dirt where Elwin was buried, and it occurred to him that, even though he'd killed the wrong man, the world was none the poorer for Elwin's passing.

Where are you? Clint thought, his neck, ribs, and back aching painfully. Let's get this over with!

But as the minutes dragged on, there was no sign of Dominic. Clint lost patience. He lowered himself to the ground, and with gun clenched firmly in hand, he advanced on the cabin expecting the dogs to pour out from inside and attack him.

But no dogs and no murderer. When Clint reached the cabin's window, he peered inside and saw nothing. It was clear that Dominic Jackson and his damned dogs were gone.

The Gunsmith swore in anger, chiding himself for not making this discovery when he'd first arrived hours earlier. He went around to the front door and stepped into the cabin. It was a pigsty, filled with rotting food. The very stench of the place drove the Gunsmith back outside.

Thirty minutes later he limped back to Hurley's livery and reclaimed his horse.

"You look awful," Dud said.

"I feel worse."

"Dominic killed her, huh?"

"Yep. Had to be him. Where do you think he headed?"

"Santa Fe would be my guess. The man never had a horse so you ought to be able to overtake him by noon. Him and his dogs."

"Yeah," Clint said. "I'll try to bring him back alive."

"To be sentenced and hanged?"

"I suppose." Clint shrugged his shoulders. "That's up to a judge and jury. Maybe they'll have mercy on him seeing as he's a little touched."

"I doubt it," the old man said. "Touched or not, the man murdered a woman that a lot of folks in Big Pine liked, despite the circumstances of her past."

"Yeah," Clint said, mounting Duke. "Where's the boy?"

"He's in school."

"Tell him I'll be back."

Clint touched his heels to Duke's flanks and sent the horse galloping toward Santa Fe. The sun was already floating over the eastern trees, but he had little doubt that he could pick up Dominic's trail and quickly overtake the man.

Four hours later, Clint saw Dominic and his dogs trotting about a mile south of the road. He might have missed them entirely because of the thick forest except that the dogs spotted a jackrabbit and took up the chase with a chorus of yips and howls.

"Come on!" Clint said, reining Duke off the wagon track and into the hills.

Dominic saw him almost immediately. The big man took off after his dogs through the trees, and the Gunsmith galloped after him on his fast gelding. As he closed the gap, Clint drew his carbine from its saddle scabbard and fired a shot at the man.

Dominic, his face wild with fear, plowed into some heavy brush, and there was nothing for Clint to do but dismount and go after him. It was hard going, and Dominic was in terrific shape. Had the big man not been breaking the trail for Clint, he might have escaped. But the brush was so thick that Clint overtook and tackled the man.

Dominic cried out and belted Clint across the side of his head. The blow was wild but packed a wallop, and Clint's vision blurred for a moment. He shook the cobwebs out of his head, and when he looked up, Dominic was streaking back through the brush.

"Damn you, you're under arrest!" the Gunsmith cried.

Dominic bellowed something and kept running. Clint had a powerful urge to draw his Colt and shoot the man in the back but resisted. He was breathing hard and the new clothes that Bill Buttering had provided him with were being torn to shreds by the manzanita.

"I swear you'll hang on a choke-knot, you jug-headed bastard!"

Dominic whooped and kept running. Clint charged after him, trying to bat the brush away with his hands and forearms in order to protect his face. He was thinking that Dominic might have it in mind to steal Duke, and that really made him run his fastest.

But Dominic wasn't thinking that clearly. He shot out of the brush and kept running, now angling for some distant pines.

Torn, winded, and bleeding from a dozen scratches, Clint grabbed his saddle horn and swung onto Duke. He yanked his carbine free and rode the big man down. Duke's shoulder struck Dominic and sent him rolling. When he tried to get up and run, Clint unleashed a bullet at Dominic's feet.

"Run again and I'll cut you down!"

"I didn't kill her! I swear I didn't!"

"Yes you did," Clint said, wrapping his reins around his saddle horn and then levering another shell into his Winchester. "You wanted to go to bed with Sarah, and when she wouldn't, you got mad and stabbed her to death with your brother's knife."

"No!"

"Yes," Clint said. "That's exactly what happened."

"Elwin killed her!"

"Your brother hated women. He wouldn't have anything to do with them. Everyone knew that. It was *you*, Dominic. You're the one that lusted for the Mexican girls up in Santa Fe. You were in need of something to poke, and after Sarah was raped by the deputies, somehow you figured that she wouldn't mind being raped just one more time. Isn't that it?"

"No!"

"It's true," Clint said, his voice hardening. "I'm charging you with the murder of Sarah Taylor."

Dominic began to shake like a wet dog. Clint didn't tell the man that all the evidence against him was circumstantial because he had no doubt that he finally had his killer.

"If you wanted a woman," Clint said, dismounting, "why didn't you go on back to Santa Fe and use one that you'd used before?"

"They don't want to see me no more!"

"Sarah didn't want you either," Clint said, leading Duke up to the man and then smashing Dominic with the butt of his Winchester.

The big man crashed to the ground, spitting teeth and blood. His broken lips quivered in terror. "You gonna kill me?"

"I wish I could," Clint said. "I could shoot you right now, and no one would be the wiser. I could say you resisted arrest and I had no choice but to put an end to your miserable life."

"Please!" Dominic began to whimper. "He told me Miss Taylor was good. He said that she would like to have me. He said she liked me!"

Clint lowered the rifle. "What are you talking about?"

"The sheriff! He said she'd let me do it if I give her a silver dollar. He gave me one. See?"

As Clint watched, Dominic hauled a silver dollar out of his pocket. The man held it up like a child and begged, "You can have the sheriff's dollar, Gunsmith. You take it and let me go!"

Clint turned away for a moment, unable to stomach the sight of this groveling, murdering half-wit. He tried to block out the sound of Dominic's pleading voice. He felt the man pressing the silver dollar against his hand, and he pulled back with disgust.

"So, Sheriff Mintner gave you that and told you to use it to pay for Sarah. That's the story, huh?"

"But she didn't want it! Instead, she got mad. Real mad. I threw it at her, and she tried to hurt me." Dominic covered his face and sobbed. "I'm sorry I stabbed her. She just made me so mad! She called me names and scratched my face. I stabbed her hard."

"Son of a bitch," Clint whispered, slapping the silver dollar away so that it went spinning into some nearby manzanita and was lost. "Dominic, we're going back to town, and you're going to tell this story in front of some witnesses, and then before a judge and jury. Maybe they'll have mercy on you—I don't know and don't much care."

"Please. Don't hang me!"

"You let me kill Elwin. You could have spoken up. You're just smart enough to know what was going on.

You could have said something, but you didn't, and Elwin died for a murder that you committed."

"He was mean to me! He hated me most as much as he hated women!"

"That doesn't surprise me. But it sure didn't give you any excuse to let him die."

When Dominic said nothing, Clint tugged down his Stetson and glared at the man. "You're responsible for the deaths of two people, Dominic. As far as I'm concerned, you deserve to be hanged."

Dominic began to cry, and the Gunsmith remounted Duke. "Let's go."

"My dogs! What about my dogs?"

"Let 'em eat the jackrabbits," Clint said, feeling miserable as he waved his gun at the man and drove him like an ox toward Big Pine. "Let 'em catch and eat the damn jackrabbits."

NINETEEN

When Clint returned to Big Pine riding Duke with Dominic trudging along in front with his head down and his hands tied behind his back, a large crowd quickly gathered.

"Did he do it? Did Dominic kill Sarah?"

These were the questions that people kept asking over and over as Clint led his prisoner toward the sheriff's office. Clint had no choice but to keep saying, "That's for a judge and jury to decide. Make way! Step aside!"

As he passed the window of the sheriff's office, Clint looked in to see if Mintner was waiting with a shotgun aimed at the door. But the office was empty, and so Clint opened the door and led his prisoner inside.

"Hold it right there," he said, going to the sheriff's desk and finding the cell keys. A moment later, he had the cell open and was shoving the big man inside.

Dominic turned and grabbed the cell bars. "I don't want to hang," he choked. "Please don't let them hang me!"

"If you testify that Sheriff Mintner said Miss Taylor would welcome your advances, then perhaps you'll receive mercy. But that's not for me to say."

Dominic swallowed noisily and shuffled over to a wooden pallet. He lay down and turned his face to the wall. Clint could hear him sobbing.

Bill Buttering stepped into the office with his daughter. They looked upset, and when they saw Clint's scratched face and arms, his new clothes in tatters, Buttering exclaimed, "What the hell happened to you?"

"I had to chase him through the brush," Clint said. "It's already been a long day."

Buttering hobbled over to the cell. "I can't wait to see you hang, you crazy, murderin' bastard!"

"Leave him alone!" Angie cried. "Can't you see he's already broken in mind and spirit? What good is yelling at him going to do for Sarah?"

Buttering deflated. "Yeah," he whispered. "But all the same, you can bet that I'll be smiling when they drop that big son of a bitch through the gallows floor."

Angie turned away and went over to Clint. "Allen is sending for gunmen," she said. "He's vowed to have you shot on sight."

The Gunsmith wasn't surprised to hear this bit of sobering news. "Has he got any help here yet?"

"No. But they're on their way."

"In that case," Clint said, "it's time to settle this issue once and for all."

"What does that mean?"

"Figure it out for yourself," Clint snapped. "Your fiancé gave Dominic a silver dollar and told him that Sarah Taylor wanted him to make love to her."

"No!"

"Yes."

"Allen wouldn't do that!."

"The hell he wouldn't," Clint said. "He wanted her punished for befriending me, for defying him."

Angie shook her head.

"He gave her a killer," Clint said cuttingly. "He put Dominic up to murdering her."

"You can't prove that!" Angie raged. "It's just your own half-baked theory."

Clint shook his head. "You just can't see the truth of things, can you? Al Mintner is rotten to the core. He knew the Jackson brothers better than anyone. He hired them all the time, and he hatched up this scheme. He set Dominic up for something that the man wasn't prepared to handle. He knew that Sarah would be enraged when that man propositioned her with a silver dollar. And he knew that she'd say something hurtful and angry. And finally, Mintner knew Dominic enough to predict that the man would explode in a killing rage."

Angie paled. "I . . . I don't know about any of that," she whispered. "It's just your theory! You could be wrong."

"You know better," the Gunsmith said. "And when Dominic goes to trial, so will a jury."

"Not in this county."

"What does that mean?"

"It means that Allen has too much influence. You'll never get a conviction."

The Gunsmith looked to his friend. "Is that right, Bill?"

"I'm afraid so," the store owner said quietly. He wheeled around and started to leave.

"Where are you going?" Angie cried.

"I'm going to get my gun and shoot Mintner like I should have done a long, long time ago."

"No!" Angie cried.

Clint strode across the office and grabbed Bill by the shoulder. "I'm the acting sheriff, remember? Bringing Mintner to justice is my job, not yours."

"You've done far more than anyone could expect. It's my turn now."

"No," Clint said. "And if you won't start acting reasonable, then I'll jail you. Bill, I swear I'll throw you in the cell with Dominic."

"You wouldn't."

"Try me," Clint said, without batting an eyelid.

Buttering took a deep breath and expelled it slowly. "All right. But this time, can I at least come along to help you arrest that rattlesnake?"

Clint didn't have the heart to say no again. "All right. But only if you promise to stay in the background and not do a thing unless I say so. Agreed?"

"Agreed," the man said with reluctance.

"I want to come, too!" Angie insisted. "After all, Allen and I are engaged. I want to know beyond question if he really put Dominic Jackson up to murder."

The Gunsmith was losing patience. "Do you actually think that he'll admit to putting Dominic onto Sarah Taylor knowing it would result in her murder?"

Angie looked away. "I just have to be there," she said in a broken voice. "Please."

The Gunsmith surprised even himself when he said, "All right. But you must promise to stay with your father at all times. And you both have to understand that Mintner is a man riding the edge of a blade and he might decide to shoot me. If he does, bullets are going to fly, and I don't want to be responsible for either of you getting shot."

"He wouldn't shoot me," Angie said. "He *loves* me without question."

"Well, he sure as hell doesn't love me," Bill Buttering growled. "And I'm going to be packing a gun—just in case everything goes to hell in a hand basket."

"That might be a very good idea," Clint said.

Clint wasn't too happy about the Butterings tagging along, but he figured that he did need some backup and that it was about time that Angie understood Mintner's true nature. No doubt the rich man's charm, power, and money had blinded her against his viciousness.

"Let's go," he said, opening the door and stepping outside to see a large crowd. "Damn."

Mr. Peterson, the local saddle maker, stepped forward and cleared his throat. "Mr. Adams," he said, "we're going to hold Big Pine's election. You and Bill Buttering are on the ballot, as sheriff and mayor, respectively."

"All right," Clint said, not in the mood for this discussion.

"Well then," Peterson said, looking pleased, "I think that about settles the issue. Some of us weren't too damn sure that you'd accept the nomination."

"I will accept it," Clint said, "but only until a qualified local man can be found. That needs to be understood."

"Sure." Peterson looked over his shoulder at the other people, then he addressed Bill Buttering. "We know that you're a sure thing for mayor, Bill. We're just a little worried about what Mr. Mintner is going to do when he finds out that he's been voted out of office and that you'll be opposing his every move."

"It won't matter," Buttering said, speaking to everyone. "Right now, acting Sheriff Adams is about to arrest Al for . . ." He looked to Clint. "What charge?"

"Uh . . . conspiracy," Clint said. "Conspiracy to murder Sarah Taylor."

On hearing this, the crowd began to buzz with excitement even as Clint took Angie's arm and steered her toward the Mintner Mansion. Bill had to struggle to keep up. Spread out behind them trailed most of the townspeople. Clint wished he could order them all to go back about their business, but he knew that they'd awaited this momentous showdown for years and would not be denied.

The townspeople's excitement was not unlike the mood that preceded a hanging.

When they reached the mansion, Clint halted and said, "Angie, you and your father stay right here and wait."

"But . . ."

"I mean it," Clint said. "I expect that Mintner will shout and raise hell, but when he realizes there is an entire crowd outside waiting to see him arrested, he'll have little choice but to come peacefully."

"I think he'd rather die than be humiliated that way," Angie said. "I don't think he'll come peacefully at all."

Clint studied the big, two-story mansion, then shrugged his shoulders. "We're going to find out real quick."

He crossed the street and went directly to the front door. It was unlocked. Throwing open the door, he shouted, "Mintner! You're under arrest!"

When there was no answer, Clint drew his six-gun, crossed the foyer, and stopped at the foot of the staircase.

"Mintner, it's Clint Adams! Come downstairs under your own steam. If I have to come after you, someone is going to get hurt."

No answer. Clint cussed in silence. Nothing ever came easy. He started climbing the stairs, and when he reached the upstairs landing, he tiptoed to Mintner's bedroom door. Pressing his ear to the door, he couldn't hear a sound. Clint placed his hand on the doorknob and turned it slowly. Like the front door, this one was also unlocked.

Taking a deep breath and sure that Mintner was waiting to kill him the moment he stepped inside, Clint jumped aside, kicking the door open. The blast of a double-barreled shotgun ripped the door to splinters. Smoke billowed from the room, and Clint threw himself to the carpet, six-gun up and firing. There was so much smoke that the Gunsmith had no target, but he wasn't giving Mintner one either as he rolled sideways and fired twice more.

The room was empty. Clint knew it the instant he saw the shotgun lashed across the arms of a chair and saw the twine that had rigged its triggers to fire when the door was knocked open. Clint jumped to his feet, batting at the gun smoke as if it was a swarm of pesky flies.

A quick search of the room told him that Al Mintner had cleared out just minutes earlier. A cigar still burned in an ivory ashtray. Wheeling around, Clint charged down the stairway and ran outside. Spotting young Dan Hurley, he shouted, "Bring me my horse—Mintner is gone!"

The crowd's reaction was surprising. They burst into cheers, and a few even broke into a jig to celebrate. Buttering said, "He'll be heading to Santa Fe for help. He'll be hiring gunfighters."

"I won't give him that edge," Clint said, turning and striding toward the livery because every moment lost gave Mintner a longer lead.

Duke was saddled and bridled in minutes. Without saying a word to anyone, Clint swung into the saddle and went racing toward Santa Fe. No one had to tell him how crucial it was that he overtake Mintner before the man reached that famous old freighting town and bought himself another small army of hired guns.

TWENTY

Late that afternoon, the Gunsmith spotted Mintner galloping northeast. He judged the horseman to be about two miles ahead. It was impossible to use the geography in order to sneak up and overtake Mintner, so Clint just dogged the man for the next few hours, steadily closing ground until Mintner happened to twist around in his saddle and spot him.

The ex-sheriff of Big Pine spurred his mount into a run, and Clint pushed Duke into an easy canter. For the next mile, he fell behind, but as Mintner's horse began to tire, Duke seemed to get stronger. This was not the first time the black gelding had been on a manhunt and understood the game.

The next two miles unfolded as Clint expected. With a winded horse, Mintner found himself losing ground and punishing his flagging mount. Even from a mile away, Clint could see that the rich man's horse was becoming heavily lathered.

When Clint narrowed the gap to a thousand yards, Allen Mintner knew that it was pointless to try to outride his pursuer. He chose a rise of ground and dismounted, dragging his rifle from its saddle scabbard.

Clint reined his horse to a standstill and yanked out his own rifle. His greatest concern was that one of Mintner's shots would strike Duke, so he turned the gelding loose and began walking toward the man.

Mintner took aim and fired, but his shot was a good five feet wide. Clint saw it kick up a spray of dirt and grass, and that told him that the ex-sheriff was not a particularly good rifleman.

The Gunsmith kept walking. Mintner's second shot was much closer, and Clint guessed he'd pushed his luck as far as possible. Dropping belly to the grass, he stretched his Winchester out before him, took aim, and fired.

Mintner screamed as the Gunsmith's slug spun him completely around, spilling the rifle from his hands. The man ran for his horse, but another well-placed bullet between the exhausted animal's forefeet caused it to bolt.

"That's far enough!" Clint shouted, coming to his feet.

Mintner's left arm dangled at his side. He turned around to face the approaching Gunsmith and waited, feet braced wide apart.

When Clint was about forty feet away, Mintner said, "You talked to Dominic Jackson. Whatever he said, he's a liar."

"He said that you put him up to killing Sarah Taylor."

"That's a damned lie!"

"No it isn't," Clint said. "You knew that she'd scorn the man and he'd lose his temper and kill her. You knew it as sure as we're all alone out here."

"Tell that to a judge and jury!" Mintner sneered. "That's all speculation; you know that it won't stand up in a court of law."

The Gunsmith thought of Sarah Taylor, remembered the warmth of her touch and the way she'd smiled. "I'm the judge and jury right now," Clint said, his face hard, his voice flat and uncompromising. "And I pronounce you guilty."

Mintner swallowed hard and looked down at his wounded left arm which dripped steadily, blood soaking into the dirt beside his boots.

"Look, I can pay you more money than you've ever imagined earning. We'll bandage this arm and ride on to Santa Fe. I'll pay you . . . a thousand dollars."

"No thanks."

"Ten thousand!"

"Not for sale."

Mintner cursed bitterly. "What do you want? More? All right, name your price!"

When Clint said nothing, Mintner's eyes tightened. "Maybe it's time that I did move back to Santa Fe. Hell, you can have my mansion. And Angie. Take 'em both!"

The Gunsmith chuckled. "So, you'd give me ten thousand dollars, your mansion, and Miss Buttering. Is that right?"

"Yeah. And you could go right on collecting protection money from the businesses. Hell, with your reputation, it'd be easy. In a year you'd own whatever I don't in Big Pine."

Mintner forced a grin. "I'm handing you the world on a damned silver platter! You'd have everything a man could dream of—money, a big house, and a beautiful wife—or mistress—if you aren't the marrying kind. Angie is good, Clint. She's as good in the sack as Sarah was in her prime. And you know how frisky Sarah was with a man."

"Yeah." Clint's hand moved closer to his gun. "I'd have everything except my self-respect. And the only way I can keep that is to see that you hang by the neck."

Mintner heaved a deep, shuddering sigh. "All right," he said, "you win! I'll return with you to Big Pine. Hell, why shouldn't I? I *own* the territorial judge. And you won't find twelve men who have the backbone to convict *me* of conspiracy to any damn murder."

Mintner grinned and raised his right hand in surrender as he came toward the Gunsmith. "You're a fool, Adams. You just threw away the offer of your lifetime. And me? Why, I'll be back in office inside of the month, and I'll keep Angie, my money, and my mansion. And what will you have?"

He snorted with cruel derision. "Not a damned thing! You'll ride out of Big Pine just as poor as you rode in."

"Some men aren't destined to have a lot of money," Clint said. "I'm resigned to that fact."

"You think you're noble, Adams, but you're not. Instead, you're just stupid."

"Shut the hell up!" Clint ordered, feeling his temper starting to fray.

"Arrest me!" Mintner laughed. "Help is already on the way to Big Pine."

That remark brought the Gunsmith up short. "You've probably agreed to pay a back-shooter or two a lot of blood money to gun me down, huh?"

"That's right. I should have hired them the first day I laid eyes on you instead of relying on my three worthless deputies."

"We all make mistakes," Clint said. He started to reach for Mintner's holstered six-gun when the man raised his wounded arm and plucked a derringer from his vest. Clint's own hand streaked for his Colt, and the two weapons roared in unison.

The Gunsmith felt the flame of death singe his belly as he fired a second round into the rich man's body. Mintner's face was only inches from his own, and he saw the man's eyes bulge with astonishment, then confusion.

"Like I said, we all make mistakes," Clint repeated as he stepped back and watched Allen Mintner pitch face first into the road.

Exactly a week later, newly elected Sheriff Clint Adams and a half dozen of Big Pine's leading citizens stepped off the boardwalk and blocked the path of two hired gunmen who drew their horses to an abrupt halt.

"What the devil is going on?" one of the men hissed. "Sheriff Adams, we ain't done nothing."

"How'd you know my name?"

"Why . . . we just heard you was hereabouts."

"I'll just bet you did, from Mintner. Now turn those horses around and ride back to whatever hole you crawled out of."

The two men exchanged glances, and the second one said, "This is a free country. A man can ride wherever he wants."

"That's a fact," Clint said. "But as you can see, you and anyone else that Allen Mintner hired just aren't welcome in Big Pine."

"I reckon we'll need to talk to Mr. Mintner about that."

"Sure," Clint said agreeably. "You can have a word with him at the cemetery on your way out. Or, if you're ready to die, you can pay Mintner a permanent visit. Your choice."

"He's dead?"

"That's right."

The bigger and uglier of the pair squinted down at Clint. "Adams, I saw you in a gunfight over in Tucson about three years ago. I'm thinking you must have slowed down a little since then. Maybe you aren't as fast as your reputation anymore. Huh?"

"Maybe you'd like to find out right now," Clint said with a slow grin.

The man looked deep into Clint's eyes and then shook his head. "Naw, I don't think I will," he said, reining his horse around and riding back the way he'd come.

"What about you?" Clint asked the second hard case.

"Gunsmith, I never seen you draw, and I'd like to see if you're as fast as they say . . . but I think there are just some things in a man's life he's best not to learn."

"You're smarter than you look. Now ride and never come back."

The gunman nodded. His cold eyes passed beyond the town to follow the Gila River across the green, verdant valley and the surrounding blue mountains. The eyes seemed to miss nothing and came to rest on Angie Buttering.

"Damn pretty town. Pretty valley. Damn pretty girl. I'd like to stay awhile."

"Not a chance," Clint said. "Not unless you go for that gun right now."

The horseman clucked his tongue with regret. He smiled at Angie and tipped his hat to her, then he reined his horse and set it to galloping back up the road toward Santa Fe.

Watch for

WEST TEXAS SHOWDOWN

144th in the exciting GUNSMITH series
from Jove

Coming in December!